The Door's Shadow

By:

Rory Milligan

The Get It Factory

The Get It Factory

www.thegetitfactory.com

THE DOOR'S SHADOW

RORY MILLIGAN

The Door's Shadow

Published by:

The Get It Factory
2154 E. Emerson Ave
Salt Lake City, UT 84108

Author - Rory Milligan
Editor - Jessica Douglas
Artwork/Design - The Get It Factory

ISBN - 978-1-953011-04-6

*To my grandparents, Pete and Lorna Scott,
without whom I would have missed this
opportunity to have my voice heard.*

*To my mom, Krista,
and my brothers, Will and Cole,
who have loved and supported me all along
the way.*

Prologue

A **PALE WOMAN WALKED ALONG A DESERTED STREET.**
Everything was silent. Her long, black hair shimmered down
her back, making her almost invisible in the night. She didn't
bother to keep to the sidewalks. She figured that the people here knew better than to risk coming near her. Even a
scrawny cat sensed her powerful aura, almost inhuman, as it
hissed and scurried down an alleyway, fur on end. The woman's face was expressionless. She kept her eyes straight ahead.
Suddenly, she stopped and spoke aloud. Her voice was cold.
"Zachary. How nice of you to join me."

From behind her, a tall man stepped out of the shadows.
"Xanedur. You know you shouldn't be here. People are starting to know what you are."

Xanedur still didn't turn around. Sounding bored, she

said, "So?"

"So," Zach answered impatiently, "you know what they'll do to you."

"Funny, you're acting like you actually care about me," Xanedur scoffed, finally turning to look at him with narrowed eyes. "Tell me, dear, is it a sin for me to want to see our children?"

Zach looked away uncomfortably. "How did you find them?"

"They don't know how to close the doors yet." An uncertain look came over her face. "They're still scared."

His gaze wandered back to her, sad and longing. Then it hardened again as he growled, "Should they not be?"

Xanedur's eyes became like shards of ice. She hissed, "That's not what you were saying a couple of years ago. What changed? Absolutely nothing!" Looking away, hiding the hint of tears, she added, "I'm still the same me."

"You tricked me," Zach accused, his voice rising.

A light came on in a nearby house, putting a pause to their argument. An indistinct face looked out the window, but upon seeing Xanedur, the face disappeared again and the light was quickly extinguished.

Xanedur, still keeping the tears at bay, turned eyes like steel back at Zach. "Can you blame me? All I wanted was a family." Her voice remained level.

There was a long moment of silence that could have lasted an eternity during which they glared at each other with a mixture of hatred and desire.

Finally, Zach took a deep breath and exhaled again. "Leave my children alone. I've warned you." He turned to leave, then hesitated. Glancing over his shoulder, he added, "For your own sake."

Xanedur watched him walk away until he was out of earshot. A tear escaping her eye at last, she murmured to herself, "You clearly never knew me at all, my love." Brushing away the tear, she continued on her way down the abandoned street. Her face, once cold, now held a shadow of grief. Everything was quiet once again.

Eventually, she came to a stop beside a small house that was hidden behind an overgrown hedge. Peering through the hedge, a thoughtful look came into her eyes, her sorrow replaced by determination. Then she began to grow dark, her body fading until she'd become a thin trail of black mist that slowly made its way through the hedge and under the front door of the house. She, in this form, was almost invisible as she floated along the ground.

It was silent in the house except for the faint clicking of a clock. Xanedur paused for a moment, considering which way to go, and then she flowed into the next room, where two cribs stood on opposite walls. The mist bunched together and became more opaque until Xanedur, in her human form, was standing in the middle of the room. Without turning on the lights, she looked fondly in one crib and then in the other.

"Hello, my children," she whispered with a wistful smile.

One of the babies began to cry, a loud noise that echoed throughout the desolate house. Alarmed, Xanedur moved to stand beside the crib. She motherly hushed the baby, but the baby's wails only grew louder.

Just as Xanedur was reaching into the crib, a door opened somewhere in the house. She froze. With one last longing look at the baby, she once again faded to mist and left the house undetected, swirling underneath the door just as quick footsteps approached.

As Xanedur fled the house, a woman entered the room and rushed to the crib. Cradling the baby, she cooed, "There, there, Rachel. Hush now. You're safe here."

Chapter 1

HIGH ABOVE LIZ'S HEAD, THE DOORS JOINED TOGETHER IN an elegant, pointed arch. Their color was a faded, dull black, as if they'd been neglected for a long time. Liz was on a marble landing, smooth steps leading down along the inside of a large, dark cave. The air was stuffy, smelling strongly of damp earth. Deep green vines curled along the grimy walls of the cave, latching themselves onto and around the doors. Small buds protruded from the vines at irregular intervals, light green and vibrant. A shadowy curtain of sorts shut off Liz's view of the rest of the cave.

A light breeze ruffled her black hair, and the vines quivered. It was almost as if they were aware of what was going to happen next. Liz knew what was coming. The wind picked up, starting to whip her hair in her eyes. She tried to move toward the stairs, but her muscles were stiff, refusing to budge even slightly.

With a feeling of dread, she watched helplessly as the doors began to shiver. A low rumble came from the doors, quiet at first, but steadily getting louder. Covering her ears didn't cut out the ominous sound. As the doors began to shake harder, the buds on the vines shuddered. They burst into red roses. Fluttering in the wind, the doors seeming as if they were about to burst open, the roses fell off of the vines and rested for a moment around Liz's feet.

She found that she could finally move her legs. Without hesitation, she flew down the stairs, jumping down two at a time into the darkness below.

Her eyes snapped open. She could hear her pulse in her ears, feel it in her eyes as she stared at her bedroom ceiling. Beads of sweat slowly traveled down the sides of her pale face, and for a few moments, she felt submerged in fear, the image of the doors still vivid in her mind. Then she heard something, a metallic clatter in the kitchen. The noise brought her back to the real world.

Closing her eyes in relief, she took a few deep breaths. As she wiped the sweat off of her face, she was briefly reminded of her father's cool hand on her forehead. Sometimes she thought about his disappearance, eleven years ago, when she was four. The touch of his hand was all she really remembered of him. Pushing the thought of him to the back of her mind, she went out to face her mother and brother, Alina and Liam.

The doors always made her feel small and vulnerable. It was almost as if her soul itself was exposed to whatever was inside. But what was inside, she didn't know. They never quite opened, though they would shake and tremble as if something on the inside were trying to get out. They were in many of her dreams. Though she was used to seeing them by now, they always inspired the same fear in her heart. She couldn't explain why they scared her so much.

Alina and Liam already knew about her chronic night-mares about the doors. They would understand if she looked shaken when she came out of her room. It was an unspoken sympathy as they would gently rest their hand on her shoulder for a moment. But for the time being, all Liz wanted was to forget about the doors, so she made sure she looked presentable before leaving her room.

Liz lived in a small town named Koln. It technically was classified as a village due to its small population. Mountains rose in the distance to the north and east. Flat plains went as far as the eye could see to the south and west, where eventually they met the coast on the southern tip of the Alorian Peninsula. The Alorian Peninsula was named for Alyspar's capital, Aloria. Aloria was in a bay on the coast a few days' travel – on horseback – to the north.

While cars had become a popular form of transportation in central Alyspar, south of the Southern Peaks had yet to create roads for cars to drive on. All they had were trails where horses with wagons could traverse. It didn't matter much that they didn't have roads though. Everyone in Koln was too poor to afford a car anyway.

The school was a small building, ten classrooms for ten grades. Liz, being fifteen, was in the seventh grade, where magic was first introduced. However, Liz had been unable to perform magic for as long as she could remember. Liam was gifted, able to create fire before even being in school. In fact, he'd nearly caught their house on fire at one point. Liz envied his natural abilities, especially every time she had to stay after school for private lessons with her teacher.

She trailed along behind Liam now as they walked the short distance to the school. Her wandering eyes came to rest on the Old People's Home, which served as both a nursing home and a hospital. A good portion of Koln's population lived there, too old or sick to take care of themselves. In the building, one of the curtains twitched, drawing her attention. An old, dark-skinned woman was staring out at her. Feeling uneasy, Liz fixed her eyes back ahead, trying to ignore the woman's scowl.

The old woman was one of the most delirious occupants of the Home, a fact well-known by everyone in Koln. Unable to recall her actual name, she called herself the Prophet, and oftentimes claimed to read the future. No one was allowed to visit her, and no one knew where she'd come from or who she'd been in her younger years. Liz had been there when she'd stumbled into Koln. The Prophet had been starving, dehydrated, and too exhausted to walk by herself. That was almost nine years ago, but the memory was clear in Liz's mind still. The peculiarity of the Prophet's arrival had been enough to stick.

As Liz watched from the corner of her eye, the Prophet's face vanished behind the curtain.

"Now, Elizabeth, just focus all of your energy into your hands, and then –" A small glow emitted from her teacher's hands. Light was one of the most basic spells, the first one taught in schools. "Once you have it," he continued, "it becomes second nature." Her teacher brought his hands to his sides, and the light faded. "Go ahead and try again."

An angry, concentrated look came over Liz's face as she tried to focus only on her hands, balled up together in front of her. She strained her entire body, trembling for a few seconds, before she let out a huge breath and relaxed.

"I just can't do it!" she cried in exasperation, crossing her arms and scowling. "I just don't know how – I don't understand…"

Her teacher frowned. In the background, the clock continued to tick. It showed that it had been almost an hour since the school day had ended. This wasn't Liz's first magic lesson. In fact, she'd been having magic lessons since the beginning of the year, which was almost two-thirds of the way through now. And yet she wasn't able to even create light.

"Elizabeth," her teacher sighed. "You'll get it," he promised with a forced smile. "With some people, it just takes time. I think it's time to be done today, though."

Liz muttered thanks and left, still feeling thoroughly

irritated and confused. First of all, she knew her teacher had meant to make her feel better, but he clearly pitied her. This made her angry. She didn't want anyone to feel sorry for her. It made her feel embarrassed. As for why she felt confused... She felt like she didn't fit in. No one else had such trouble with magic. She couldn't figure out what she was doing wrong, what she should change. Feeling isolated and alone, she hardly noticed the havoc around the Old People's Home.

Several people were rushing around outside of the Home, running with panicked expressions. As Liz watched, none other than the Prophet burst from the doors, her eyes wide as she frantically scanned the outside area. Then her eyes pinned on Liz. She froze as the Prophet began to sprint toward her, moving faster than Liz would have thought was possible for the old woman.

The Prophet tripped, giving the people outside just enough time to restrain her. The Prophet screamed while they shouted to each other indistinctly. Then she was under control, one person each holding her arms. They steered her back inside while she shrieked and kicked. Liz heard what the Prophet was yelling, the words chilling her to the bone.

"I need to talk to her! They're coming, they're –" Before she could finish her sentence, they'd managed to get her back inside of the building, and her shouts faded. Shaken, Liz gingerly walked past the Home. People dissipated, casting Liz uncertain looks. With their eyes on her, she felt even more like an outcast.

Liz's eyes darted between the windows. She was almost

past the Home when the curtains behind one window were yanked out of the way, and the Prophet's face appeared. She was shouting something, staring directly at Liz still and beating the window with her weak fists. Liz stopped again, her heart pounding, her mind going blank.

"Chosen!" the Prophet cried, her voice quietly carrying from inside the Home. "It's her! Let me talk to her!"

Suddenly the Prophet was pulled away from the window. One of the caretakers glanced out to see Liz. Their eyes met for a split second, and then the caretaker disappeared, presumably trying to calm down the Prophet. Her whole body tense, Liz fled back to her house, her failed attempts to create light almost completely forgotten.

Liam chuckled when Liz told him about the Prophet's escape from the Home. "You're kidding. She hasn't left that place in years, why would she now?" He paused as he caught sight of Liz's somber face. "You okay?"

"It's just… It was disturbing." Liz's voice was quiet as she added, "She was looking right at me. You didn't see her."

"I'm sure it's fine. She's gotten out of there, what, once in nine years? They'll have her on lockdown now." His smile faded, and then he cleared his throat. "So how did your magic lesson go?"

Trying to put the Prophet at the back of her mind, Liz scowled. "Terrible. I still can't even make light."

Liam looked thoughtful for a moment and then said, "Maybe you just need some motivation. Maybe if you're in a dark place – I could even just turn off the lights in here…" He walked to the wall and flipped the switch. They were plunged into darkness. "Now try," Liam instructed.

Liz put her hands together in front of herself and concentrated, straining every muscle in her body. She imagined holding lights, trying to focus her energy into her hands, but when several seconds passed with no results, she gave up. "I'll never get it."

Magic had been the one thing Liz had looked forward to learning about in school. The ability to conjure light, fire, ice, or even darkness itself was appealing to her, or the skill of healing. The school only taught the basic versions of these spells. They avoided darkness altogether. The power to manipulate and create darkness was considered dark magic, once used by demons who roamed the countryside, terrorizing the innocent. The magic used by the demons was illegal in Alyspar.

Demons hadn't been spotted near Koln for years upon years. Liz had never even heard of one being sighted, and the history books in school didn't contain much about them. It made sense that she wouldn't have heard of one causing trouble though, as Koln was very isolated from the rest of Alyspar. Not much news came south of the Southern Peaks.

The teachers didn't like to discuss demons, and Alina especially tended to avoid the subject. If Liz brought demons up, Alina would scoff and insist that those who claimed to be tormented by them were either crazy or superstitious. "Demons are long gone," she'd say with an annoyed sigh. "Stop thinking about a past you weren't present for."

Several days later, Alina came home to find Liz and Liam sprawled out on the living room couch. Liam was juggling a fireball, grinning at Liz occasionally. Liz watched enviously. Alina's eyes flashed, and she snapped, "Hey, no fire in the house! You know the rules." The fire in Liam's hands vanished and he looked at her apologetically. She added, "You remember what happened last time."

"Sorry, Mom, I was just trying to show Liz a trick."

"You were not," Liz scoffed, sitting up. "You just wanted to show off!"

"Did not!" Liam scowled and looked away.

Liz smiled, amused, and looked back at Alina. Liz's smile faded. Alina's usual positive expression was not there. In its place was a slight frown, a wistful look in her eyes. Liz blinked, and almost immediately Alina's eyes had cleared. She nudged Liz's feet out of the way to sit on the couch with them.

"How was school?" Alina started to ask, but a loud knock at the door interrupted her. She looked at the door, her face dark. Liam began to stand up, but Alina lightly pushed him back down, saying, "I'll get it." As she walked to the door, Liz and Liam exchanged curious looks at their mother's odd behavior.

Alina glanced back at them before answering the door, only opening it wide enough for her to be able to see outside. Liz leaned around, trying to catch a glimpse of whoever was at the door. Alina's words were too quiet to hear at first, but then suddenly her voice rose in a hiss. "I'm not going to see her again, and you tell her to leave my children alone!" She slammed the door, making Liz flinch. Alina didn't turn around at first, and for a few moments they sat in tense silence. Finally, Liam ventured to ask what that was all about.

Their mother drew in a long breath and turned around, a stiff smile on her face. "It's nothing for you to worry about," she assured them, but she didn't rejoin them on the couch. Instead, she walked to the kitchen to start making an early dinner.

That night, the doors came up in Liz's dreams again. She stood facing them as usual. However, this time she was not alone. With a sidelong glance, she contemplated the strange fondness she seemed to feel for the teenage boy next to her. She didn't even recognize him.

He was taller than her but only looked to be a year or two older. His pale skin contrasted with their dark surroundings. His bright, blue eyes were trained on the doors as if he were waiting for something, but his body seemed relaxed. And then he spoke.

"Do you know where we are?"

Liz shook her head.

"Do you know what these doors lead to?"

She shook her head again.

"Do you know who you are?"

Confused by now, Liz tilted her head a bit and answered,

"Of course."

"I don't think you do," the boy sighed, finally looking back at her with a raised eyebrow.

This only made Liz feel more confused. "How could I not know who I am?" As if to prove herself to him, she added, "I'm Elizabeth Prower."

The boy shook his head and gazed back at the doors with a sad look in his eyes. "That's only half of you." He turned from her and began to walk away, down the marble steps. Liz followed at his heels, determined to figure out what he meant. But as she reached for his shoulder to stop him, she realized that while her legs were moving, she was stuck in place.

"Hey," she called as the boy got farther and farther away. "Hey!"

But he didn't turn around, and soon he'd disappeared from sight completely. The doors, silent and foreboding, didn't even quiver.

When Liz woke up, her memory of the dream was hazy. She couldn't remember the boy's face. All that remained was a strange ache in her heart, as though she'd lost something very dear to her.

She wanted to be alone, but her room was making her feel trapped, reminding her of the doors. Wanting to forget about them, Liz went outside and started to walk. She hadn't gone very far before she heard a hoarse voice off to the side, saying her name. With a startled jump, Liz looked to see who'd spoken. To her surprise and discomfort, it was the Prophet.

15

The ancient woman, dark skin almost completely hidden by shawls of all colors, was in the shadows of the Old People's Home. A variety of beads were strung around her neck. The Prophet had a bony finger hooked out, beckoning Liz to come closer.

"How did you get out here?" Liz demanded suspiciously, not moving.

"Hush," the Prophet croaked, "just come here. I have something important to tell you."

Liz hesitated. The image of the Prophet screaming and trying to escape the Home a few days before was fresh in her mind. The Prophet's eyes were glittering.

"Don't you want to know what your mother's been hiding from you?"

After a few tense moments, Liz's curiosity overcame her caution. She carefully moved toward the Prophet. Once she'd reached the shadows, she stopped, still at least ten feet away from the old woman.

"What do you know?" she asked warily. The Prophet frowned.

"I can't speak that loudly, child. Step closer."

Reluctantly, Liz edged closer and leaned in.

"You, Elizabeth..." the Prophet murmured. "You are Chosen."

Liz toyed with the words in her head but wasn't sure what they meant. "Chosen for what?"

Sudden footsteps came from behind her. Suddenly, Liam was standing next to her, coldly eyeing the prophet.

"Liz, what are you doing here?"

Liz looked at the Prophet with her mouth parted, unsure of what to say. The Prophet's eyes lazily wandered to Liam for a moment before he grabbed Liz's shoulder and started to steer her back out of the alleyway.

"We should be going," he muttered.

"Wait!" the Prophet called, stepping after them. "Elizabeth, you and your brother – you are Chosen!" Liam froze and glanced back at the old woman.

"Chosen? Chosen for what?" he asked slowly, his grip on Liz's shoulder loosening. When she didn't answer immediately, he added more aggressively, "What do you mean?"

"I mean..." the Prophet wheezed, "that you will be in great danger soon." She paused for a brief second, during which her glazed eyes closed, as if she were terribly exhausted.

"What kind of danger?" Liam insisted, sounding impatient.

The Prophet's face was solemn as she answered, "The demon Xanedur has been at work recently. People are vanishing again..." she paused for a deep breath, "as they did in the dark ages. You are the only ones who stand a chance against it." The Prophet seemed to be looking at Liz in particular. Liz shifted uncomfortably.

"What does that have to do with us?" Liz asked uncertainly. She didn't want yet another thing to make her different from her classmates.

"They're looking for you. They just haven't found you yet."

"Hey!" an angry voice sounded behind them. Startled,

Liz looked over her shoulder to see Alina marching toward them, glowering at the Prophet. "What are you telling my children?"

"It's time that they knew, Alina," the Prophet whispered, her voice low. Alina gave Liz and Liam a sideways glance before pulling the Prophet aside.

"Why are you doing this to them?" Alina asked under her breath.

"You're not asking for them, you're asking for yourself," the Prophet answered, not bothering to keep her voice down. "They need to know who they are, before it's too late."

Liz and Liam exchanged a confused glance. There was an uncomfortable pit in Liz's stomach that was starting to make her feel sick. It just seemed to be getting bigger and bigger.

"Please just leave them out of this," Alina sighed. "They're just kids!"

The Prophet's eyes came to rest on Liz. "Their time is limited." Liz's blood ran cold, and she shivered. Alina followed the Prophet's gaze and was still for a moment before shaking her head.

"You're wrong," she told the Prophet with a note of finality. She rested a hand each on Liz and Liam's shoulders, pulling them away. "Stay away from my kids." And she led them back to their house, shrugging off their fearful questions. Liz caught one backwards glance of the Prophet, still peering out at them from the shadows. Then Alina had ushered her through the door.

It wasn't long after that they found out that the Prophet hadn't gone back into the Old People's Home after getting out. She was missing and hadn't been seen since she'd confronted Liz and Liam.

"Good riddance," was all Alina would say. Liz and Liam avoided the topic with each other, afraid to bring it back up. However, the Prophet's words echoed in her head, and she found herself looking over her shoulder more often than before. But with the Prophet gone and Alina stubbornly leaving the topic out of discussion, there was no one to ask any questions either Liz or Liam had, such as what the Prophet had meant when she'd said that they were Chosen… or that their time was limited.

Chapter 2

THERE WERE THE DOORS. TALL, DARK, INTIMIDATING. Silent.

A light breeze ruffled Liz's hair. The vines wrapped around the balcony and spread onto the doors. The smell of damp earth was almost overwhelming. This time, she was alone.

Her heart pounded in her chest as she stared at the doors apprehensively, but for a long time nothing stirred but the wind. She felt like if she were to move, the doors would open. So she stayed where she was, frozen with fear. Stuck on the balcony, surrounded by nothingness. After a while, she caught a strained voice in the air.

"They're coming... We've found you."

Suddenly the doors began to shake violently. Startled out of her frozen stupor, Liz rushed down the stairs, and then –

A knock on her bedroom door woke her up. Alarmed, shaking with the fresh memory of her dream, Liz slowly walked toward the door, unsure of what to expect. Before she reached it, the door opened without another warning. Liz made a strangled noise of fear – but it was just Alina. Gasping with relief, Liz closed her eyes for a moment. But when she opened them again, she realized that something about Alina's weary appearance seemed off. She looked scared, her eyes wide. Her hair was a mess as if she'd been pulling at it.

"Elizabeth," she said quietly. She never called Liz by her full name. "Get dressed. You and Liam have to come with me, okay?"

Liz, confused, started to ask her what was going on, but Alina had already moved on to Liam's door to wake him. Soon enough, Liz and Liam were following Alina outside, going toward the stables on the northern edge of Koln.

"Mom, wait..." Liz murmured tiredly. "What's going on?" She was feeling a mixture of scared urgency with having just woken up, but the scared urgency was beginning to overcome her weariness. Her heart felt like it was steadily climbing up her chest to her throat. She and Liam both were starting to feel concerned.

"You and Liam have to ride to Aloria and get to the Queen. She will protect you," Alina said quietly, almost absently, set on their destination.

"Protect us from what? Why do we have to go?" Liam yawned. They both stumbled along at Alina's fast pace.

"Somehow..." Alina paused as if the next words were

21

painful. "Somehow a powerful demon has found out that you've been here, and they're coming for you now. But once you get to Aloria, you'll be safe."

"Why are they coming for us though?" Liam asked persistently. Liz wanted to know the answer to that just as much as her brother, though she knew it wouldn't be a good one.

"There's not enough time for me to explain everything to you right now," Alina answered as they approached the stables. She turned to them, and Liz saw that her face was stained with tears. The Prophet unexpectedly appeared from inside the stables and walked toward them.

"You brought them," she said simply. She beckoned to someone inside the stables. A tall, slim man came out, leading two stout horses. Another horse was obediently waiting nearby, watching them as it pawed the ground. The man looked to be middle-aged with rough facial hair, but he had a youthful, keen look in his eyes.

"This is someone from Aloria to guide you there," Alina murmured, her voice breaking.

"He came on short notice to bring you a letter, and it's a good thing too," the Prophet said with a glance at Alina.

"What letter?" Liz asked, finally awake enough to speak coherently.

"The Queen has summoned you. That no longer matters though. You both now need to leave this place immediately, regardless of the letter." The Prophet turned to speak in a low voice with their guide, leaving them with Alina.

"I love you both, no matter what," Alina whispered, pulling

them both into a tight embrace. It dawned on Liz that Alina wasn't coming with them. They were leaving Koln behind, along with their mother.

Liz pushed Alina away to look at her. With a desperate note in her voice, she asked, "Wait, you're not coming with us?"

"These are the only two horses fit for travel, and you need to move quickly. I would just slow you down. But I will see you again," Alina promised, meeting Liz's eyes with a strained smile. "And until then, your guide and the Queen will keep you safe. Okay?"

"Wait, but – "

"Alina, time is running out," the Prophet called. "The sooner they get away from here, the better." She hunched over and broke into a coughing fit.

Alina ran her hand down the side of Liz's face, softly kissed Liam and her on their foreheads, and led them to the horses.

"Mom, we're not leaving you here!" Liz insisted, trying to pull her arm free. "Can't you –"

Liam cut in at the same time, "There has to be a way for you to come with us!"

"I told you," Alina explained patiently, "that these are the only two horses who can handle riding to the capital. It's a long ride to Aloria. You'll have to go without me. You matter more than anyone in Koln. You are Chosen."

"But –"

A shrill scream from nearby cut Liz off. They all froze for a moment before the Prophet said forcefully, "You need to go *now."*

Her own immediate fear overcame Liz's reluctance to leave Alina long enough for her to climb up onto the smaller, black horse. A loud crash sounded in the distance, and hazy smoke rose from the other side of Koln, not far off.

"Now go!" the Prophet ordered their guide as soon as Liam had climbed onto the saddle of the larger horse, white with black spots. Liz looked at their guide, the strange man, who met her eyes for a moment. Alarmed by the screams coming from nearby, smoke filling the air around them, she hardly comprehended that they were leaving Koln – and Alina. The horses were shifting nervously, snorting and letting out small whinnies.

"Just follow me," their guide said quickly. He turned his horse to face the Southern Peaks, just north of Koln. Liz gave an anguished look back at Alina, who had tears now streaming freely down her face. Another explosion sounded from nearby, closer than the first. A dim light lit up the area near them, heavy smoke settling in the area.

More screams and explosions filled Liz's ears. Screams of people she probably knew. As their guide prepared to move, the Prophet gave a hacking cough and fell down onto the ground with a thud. Their guide hesitated.

Alina, noticing him, venomously hissed, "Go!" She knelt down next to the Prophet as their guide hurriedly obliged.

Liz gripped her horse's neck tightly as they began to move, jolting up and down in time with the horse's steps. She looked over her shoulder to see Alina drop the Prophet, who wasn't responding. Alina disappeared behind the stables. A small, dark shape came out from around a corner, glancing over at Liz. Then it raced away, following Alina's trail.

"No –" Liz breathed. Things were moving in slow motion. She realized that the dark shape must have been a demon.

Smoke billowed up from Liz's hometown, flames lighting up the area. Looking forward, Liz saw the vast forest that spread across before the mountains. They were already nearing it, a lone tree growing here and there around them before the foliage would thicken. Staring back with wide eyes, hair whipping her face, she saw that the Prophet had disappeared. Standing beside the stables where they had been just moments before was a large demon. It faced them without moving. Liz could feel its hard gaze boring into her back, almost like the fire now spreading from building to building. A chill ran down her spine.

But the demon didn't move, and then they were weaving through the trees. A thicket cut off her sight for a few seconds. When she could see her burning hometown again, the demon was gone.

For a long time, no one spoke. Still in shock from leaving Koln – and Alina – on such short notice, Liz stared forward without really seeing. A glance at Liam would've shown that he felt similarly. They'd slowed down to a walk. While Liz's mood remained dark, the sun had risen, and it was mid-morning. Their guide had introduced himself. His name was Seth, and he was a Royal Guard from Aloria. The Queen had sent him to retrieve Liz and Liam. They hadn't been able to speak enough to ask why.

The last few hours had allowed Liz's mind to slowly move from one thing to another as she blankly tried to understand what had happened. She'd had that dream, heard a voice. And then suddenly, demons had come to Koln. *They're coming...we've found you.* She heard the echo of the voice over and over in her head. She couldn't tell if it had only been a dream or if it had been something more.

The image of her hometown going up in flames was burned into her mind. And the demon staring at them as they fled... She felt like it had been looking at her in particular. Blood-curdling screams sounded in her ears even now, the screams of people she had probably known. And Alina...

Suddenly she was aware that they'd stopped. They were deep in the forest by now, and the trees, grouped close together, covered up most of the sky. The forest floor was an almost constant cover of bushes and fallen trees. Around them was a small, clear area.

Now Seth looked back at Liz and Liam with a hint of pity in his eyes. "You two look like you could use some rest. We'll stop here for a few hours." They released the horses to graze. Seth pulled what looked like crackers from a saddlebag and handed some over to both of them. "We don't have a lot of food to last us these few days, so I hope you two are okay with only eating a bit. Once we get to Aloria, the Queen will see that you have more than enough to eat and drink. The Chosen are treated almost as royalty in the capital."

"What does that mean?" Liz asked, finally finding her voice. It sounded bitter and hoarse, probably from the tight feeling in her throat.

"What does what mean?" Seth asked, sounding confused.

"'Chosen'. What exactly does that mean?"

Seth, still seeming confused, answered, "People who are Chosen are stronger against demons than the average person. They're better with dark magic." At Liz and Liam's blank expressions, he added, "Which, you know, it's the only magic that really works against demons."

"I thought dark magic was illegal," Liam inserted.

"Not for Chosen, as long as it's used against demons. It's necessary for them to learn how to use it before they fight greater demons."

"A greater demon? As opposed to what?" Liam asked. Liz, still trying to process everything, was quiet.

"As opposed to a lesser demon. Greater demons are the... big guys, the ones with all the power. They create Gates, they tell lesser demons what to do..."

"What's a Gate?" Liam questioned.

"It's a connection between our world and the demon world, the Other World – didn't your school teach you anything about demons?"

"No," Liz said distantly.

"Well then," Seth sighed, "the Queen wouldn't be too happy about that. We need as many Chosen as we can get right now."

"What makes us Chosen?" Liz asked. If she'd been more

herself, the question would have sounded fierce.

Seth shifted. "No one really knows why some people are Chosen and some aren't. We just know that the Chosen are stronger against greater demons. Chosen can handle being near a Gate. Normal people have trouble moving near them, let alone casting spells."

Liam cut in, "Why do we need Chosen right now? What's going on?"

"Demons have been very active on the other side of the Southern Peaks lately, especially near Aloria. Reports say that most of them are acting under orders from the greater demon Xanedur. We've tried fighting it, but…" He cleared his throat uncomfortably. "We sent an army of two hundred to fight it. It destroyed all but a few. My brother was among the dead." He took a deep breath, and Liz could see a hint of tears in his eyes. "Then… some lesser demons broke through the wall around Aloria a few days ago. The demons were defeated, but they caused terrible damage. Many civilians died before we were able to stop them."

Cutting through her numbness, the reality of what demons were doing to the rest of Alyspar hit Liz with a pound. Koln's separation from the rest of Alyspar had kept their influence unknown to her. Still fresh in her mind, Liz once again saw Koln going up in flames. She blinked in an attempt to make it go away, but it was burned to the back of her eyelids. Inwardly flinching, she tuned back into the conversation.

Liam was staring at Seth in disbelief. "How could one demon kill two hundred people? It's just one demon, right?"

Seth patiently explained, "Xanedur is a greater demon. Greater demons are much stronger than lesser demons, like the ones that attacked Koln. Greater demons usually stick around their Gates."

"Were the ones who went to fight Xanedur... Were they Chosen?" Liam asked shakily. Liz, mirroring his train of thought, wondered how they could make a difference when Xanedur had defeated an army of two hundred people.

"No," Seth answered. "They were ordinary people. To destroy Xanedur, we only need a few Chosen. That's why I was sent to get you two."

"You expect *us* to kill Xanedur?" Liz cut in, aghast.

Seth nodded, giving them both a pitiful look. "You don't have a choice. You're Chosen. You're some of the only people who stand a chance." He looked down for a moment. When he raised his eyes again, the pity was gone. "The Queen is sending for Chosen from all over Alyspar to help against greater demons. The situation on the other side of these mountains isn't good. But once we get to Aloria, you'll be treated like royalty while in training. You'll be more prepared than any army could be for fighting them."

Liam, seeming more confident than before, asked, "You said that greater demons could create Gates, right? Then how do lesser demons get through to our world?"

"Lesser demons use a greater demon's Gate in exchange for some type of service."

Slowly, Liam asked, "Can people go through those Gates?"

"We don't really know," Seth answered. "No one's ever

gone into the Other World before."

The doors from Liz's dreams flashed in her mind. With a sinking feeling, she suddenly had an idea of what the doors were. "What do these Gates look like?"

"Well, they can look like a lot of things… I wouldn't really know because I've never seen one. Not many people get that close and survive," Seth said uncertainly. Liz shivered. She wondered what could be behind those doors and whose voice she'd heard.

While she was lost in her own thoughts, Liam continued the conversation. "Why didn't we learn about any of this in school?"

A thoughtful look came over Seth's face. "Demons aren't usually active on this side of the mountains. Not these days. Koln is…" A pained look came over his face. "Koln *was*…so isolated that few people probably heard about the demon attacks up north. They probably just thought that demons were nothing more than stories." A few seconds passed. "It used to be bad about two hundred years ago, before Alyspar and Cujan had become two separate countries. Demons were everywhere, hidden in human disguises, killing innocent people. Then, when Alyspar was founded, a group of Chosen came together and fought against all known greater demons. Most of them were banished back to the Other World or killed. No one quite knows what happened to most of the Chosen after the war, but Alyspar was under control.

"It's gotten worse again in the last year. People traveling on the roads have been attacked, others have been disappearing.

After the demons broke through Aloria's wall... We sent scouts after the last group of demons and tracked them back to the Alysparian Peninsula, somewhere in the Dry Mountains. But we don't know exactly where the Gate is. We think they are working for Xanedur. It was causing a lot of problems about fifteen years ago, but then it disappeared. Until now. It probably sent the demons to Koln too."

With a mixture of confusion and fear, Liz looked at Seth. "So...those demons that attacked Koln... They were looking for us?"

Seth met her eyes earnestly. "Yes. They were."

It wasn't exactly unexpected that the doors were in Liz's dreams again that night. Ancient and proud, they towered above her. This time, no voice accompanied their appearance. However, the boy from before was standing in front of her, a curious look in his blue eyes as he observed her. His dark hair fluttered in the light breeze.

"Do you understand where you are now?" he asked. "I heard the voice last night."

Liz fearfully peered past him to the doors. "Is this a... Gate?"

The boy solemnly nodded. "I'm surprised you could make it here without knowing what it was before. The Cujan Cabinet had to explain everything to me for me to get here. Though I suppose Alyspar hasn't told you much about that." It was more of a question than a statement.

Liz slowly shook her head. "The Cujan Cabinet? Why

– Why am I here?"

"Because you're Chosen," the boy answered. A dark shadow crossed his face as he looked over his shoulder at the doors. "This is Xanedur's Gate. Its physical form is located in the Dry Mountains." As if a sudden thought crossed his mind, he suddenly looked back at her and asked, "Do you know who I am?"

He and the doors were beginning to go dark as she responded, confused, "No…"

The boy sighed and shook his head in frustration. "You're fading. I wouldn't be able to…" His voice faded away.

High above the trees, the sun shone between spots of clouds. Seth was already packing up their small camp. Liam was still sound asleep, but as Liz sat up, he began to stir. He leaned up on an arm and looked around in a daze. Liz stretched her stiff muscles, flinching at her soreness. She wasn't used to riding a horse for so long, nor was she used to sleeping on hard ground. She grimaced at the thought of doing this for several more days on their way to Aloria.

The horses began to whinny and pull at their leads. Seth glanced at them, listened for a moment, and hastily packed up the rest of their things, almost yanking Liz's sleeping bag away from her. "We need to hurry," he said quietly with a wary look behind them. "Get on your horses."

Liz winced as she climbed onto the saddle. Every muscle was hurting, but Seth's urgency kept her moving. There was a slight rustling in the bushes nearby. She froze, giving an uncertain glance at Seth. His wide eyes, scanning the area behind them, were enough to make Liz forget about her sore legs and back.

By now, the horses were dancing on their hooves, impatiently whimpering. Seth began to lead them away, looking over his shoulder at foliage behind them. The rustling had gotten louder. Then it suddenly stopped. Seth clicked his tongue at his horse, speeding them up a little. He still seemed apprehensive.

Without further warning, there was a loud, monstrous roar. A large bear, powerful and dark, erupted from the bushes, its eyes furious and hungry. The horses immediately reacted, reaching a gallop in the opposite direction within a second. Liz gripped onto her horse's neck, scared of falling off at the sudden movement. She could see Liam having the same reaction, his fearful eyes staring forward.

Liz's heart pounded in her chest, almost in time with the slapping of the bear's great paws upon the ground. It was picking up speed, lumbering after them ravenously. Seth's horse was overtaking their smaller horses, but he continued to watch behind them, a hand at the ready. For what, Liz didn't know. She couldn't imagine what they could do against such an angry creature.

The bear growled with rage. Liz saw with a glance behind her that it was gaining on them, jumping over fallen trees and rocks with ease. Liz heard Seth murmur something to himself. Shocking her further, a sharp shard of ice flew from his hand toward the bear, missing the brown beast by mere inches.

Coming up right behind them without a pause, the bear swatted at Liz's horse, catching it on the haunch. Her horse screamed in pain as it stumbled, nearly throwing Liz off. She let out a terrified scream and held on tighter to her horse's neck. At the same instant as the bear reared up, ready to finish off Liz's horse, a fireball hit it square in the chest, and it fell back. The bear roared in agony, falling to the ground while the fireball burned a large hole in its fur, right to its skin. Liz's horse tripped after Seth's and Liam's horses as they raced away.

It was a while before they could calm down the horses enough to stop. Once they did, Seth immediately jumped off to examine Liz and her horse. "Elizabeth, are you okay?" he demanded, eyes scanning over her and her horse's injured leg.

"What do you think?" Liz snapped, feeling fresh tears in her eyes now that they were safe. "That bear nearly killed me!"

Liam also dismounted his horse, coming over to join them. "Why didn't you do that earlier?" he growled, glaring at Seth. "That was way too close!"

"I was hoping that it wouldn't be necessary." Before saying anything else, Seth looked over the fresh wound on Liz's horse. It was breathing heavily, eyes wide and nostrils flaring as it favored its hind leg. Finally he added, "That's why I'm here. This is all going to get worse before it gets better. Well..." With a sigh, he changed the subject. "The horse can keep walking, but we won't be able to go very fast from here.

It will still be a few days before we reach Aloria."

Liz groaned, beginning to feel her sore muscles all over again now that the adrenaline was gone. She was about to say something when Seth spoke again.

"Look." His voice was patient. "I don't like riding for days on end or dealing with situations like this either. But if you tough it ouf for a few more days, we'll be in Aloria. You'll have everything you could ever dream of in the Palace. Just a few more days. Now then... We should move a bit farther before we rest again. Before that bear decides to come back for more."

Chapter 3

LIZ BLEARILY OPENED HER EYES. WITH A YAWN, SHE SAT up only to see that the horses, Seth, and Liam were all gone. Her muscles screamed in protest as she pushed herself to her feet, more sore than ever. But that was forgotten in her panic. Looking behind trees and bushes, hoping that this was just some sort of practical joke, she could see no sign of Liam or Seth. Beads of sweat from stress were forming on her face, and her heart was in her throat. Shaking, she fell to her knees at last, helpless tears in her eyes. It began to rain, drops of water mixing in with the tears rolling down her face. She let out a scared sob and buried her face in her hands, not knowing what to do.

A twig cracked behind her, and she froze. One – it could be Liam or Seth. Or two – it could be the bear. Or three – what if it was something worse?

"Liam? Seth…?" she tentatively murmured, turning around. All she saw were bushes and trees. Another twig split on her other side. She jumped, looking back forward through her tears. Then her eyes grew wide with terror.

Looming over her was a dark shape, a liquid-like shadow. It was a demon, a humanoid shape with hollow holes where the eyes should've been. Its mouth was open wide in a crooked smile with razor-sharp teeth. Its arms almost reached the ground with claws instead of fingers. Liz screamed and jumped to her feet, stumbling in the other direction. But the demon was faster. It reached toward her and engulfed her in a black shadow…

She woke with a gasp. Covered with sweat, she looked around to see that it had just been a nightmare. Liam and Seth were by the horses, packing everything up. Neither of them noticed Liz as she sat up. Her heart was hammering inside her chest, as it so often did when she woke from a nightmare. She took deep breaths, trying to calm down and relax. The dried sweat, still dampening her clothes, made her want a shower more than anything.

"Elizabeth, are you ready to go?" Seth asked when he noticed her shakily get to her feet. Obviously concerned, he glanced at Liam. Liam was staring at Liz with a frown.

"Are you okay?" he asked quietly when she approached them. "Another nightmare?"

"I'm fine," Liz muttered, still feeling the fear from her dream. "Just a dream. Let's go."

Because of the wound on her horse, Liz rode on Seth's while he walked beside them. Their pace was slow, allowing the lame horse to keep up. Even so, it stumbled over the uneven ground.

Seth kept throwing glances at Liz. She looked away uncomfortably, her eyes scanning the forested area. Finally Seth spoke. "Liam said 'another nightmare'. Do you have a lot of them?"

With a blink, Liz looked back ahead, her eyes distant. "Yeah. Almost every night."

"I've heard about some Chosen who have had nightmares that told them… things."

"What kind of things?" Liz asked, her discomfort rising.

"Just… things about demons. They're only rumors, but some people say that nightmares show the Chosen where Gates are."

Liz looked at him dubiously. "My nightmares aren't like that."

Seth shrugged and fell silent for a few moments. Then, as if unable to stop himself, changed the subject. "What's it like? Being Chosen, I mean."

"I don't… really know," Liz admitted. Finding out what it meant to be Chosen had shocked her at first, but now she felt as if nothing had changed. The day was still passing, she was still breathing. Plus she didn't know enough about being Chosen to feel much different. It wasn't being Chosen that made her feel different. But the demons… Scared and helpless against them, she felt much the same about her own fate now. Taken away from everything she'd ever known, forced to fight against Xanedur in the near future… It all felt like another nightmare. "It just feels like…" She trailed off again, not sure how to put what she felt into words.

Liam cut in, "It feels miserable." His voice, though quiet, carried to them over early evening birdsong. With a quick glance at him, Liz could see him looking straighting ahead. A soft emptiness showed in his eyes. She realized that he must be feeling like she was – lost and confused.

Trying to distract herself from her own thoughts, Liz asked Seth, "What's Aloria like?"

A fond smile crossed Seth's face, though it didn't spread to his eyes. "It's huge. So huge that you won't believe it until you see it. Buildings that are seventy, maybe eighty feet tall… People everywhere. The upper district and Palace grounds are beautiful. You'll love it."

"The upper district? Are there other districts?" Liz wondered curiously.

Sounding surprised, Seth replied, "Yeah, there's the lower district and the middle district too." As an afterthought, he added, "And the business district. That's where the really tall buildings are."

Trying to process this, Liz frowned. Coming from Koln, a small town to the south of the Southern Peaks, she didn't understand what the difference between the districts would be. She wasn't used to class differences. But, the memory of her nightmare coming back, she didn't ask anything else about the capital. Feeling forlorn once more, she fell silent.

As the next couple days pressed on, long and monotonous, the mountains in the distance had grown larger. The wound on Liz's horse looked to be infected, so they towed it along behind them while Liz continued to ride Seth's horse. Seth walked alongside them. Liz wondered if his feet hurt, but he didn't show any signs of being in pain.

It was growing dark now, and they had stopped for the day. Seth cast a watchful spell that took the form of a golden dog. The dog promptly laid down on the ground, ears erect and eyes facing forward. It didn't seem to get distracted by anything, not even their fumbling through the contents of their saddlebags.

"This spell will warn us if anything dangerous comes near," Seth explained, resisting a yawn as he sat on the ground. Liz, with a twinge, noticed him massage his feet a bit. Then he added, with a nervous chuckle, "I need sleep just like the rest of you." Despite the gray bags under his eyes, he didn't look comfortable taking a break from watching to sleep. As he laid on the ground, his eyes squinted as though he had trouble keeping them open. Mere moments later, they had closed, and he was asleep. Liz followed his lead and drifted off to sleep, trying to ignore the soreness throughout her entire body.

Against her wishes, Xanedur's Gate was there again. The boy was there again too, standing beside Liz as they faced the doors together. At least she wasn't alone this time. Turning her head to look at the boy, she saw that he was already staring at her. His mouth was moving, but no words were coming out. Liz found that her own mouth was clamped shut, and she couldn't open it to speak.

"What are you saying?" she wondered, narrowing her eyes.

As his mouth moved silently, he gestured to the doors. Liz glanced at them as they stood motionless and silent. Dull black and gloomy, as usual. Tall, at least twice Liz's height, vibrant roses blooming on dark green vines.

She looked back at the boy. He was still talking without making a sound. Then he stopped and met her eyes, reaching out a hand. Liz tentatively took it in her own and gave him a level look. Together, they turned to the doors, though Liz had no idea what to expect.

A dark murmuring sound came from the doors. A breeze picked up and ruffled the roses, sending them flying and tumbling through the air. Some stray petals fell to the marble floor. Liz was used to this routine by now, but she still paid apprehensive attention as the doors began to shake. They were quiet at first, but they were growing more violent by the second. A low shriek pierced through the air around them, and the doors began to slowly open. The shriek's pitch rose note by note until the doors were wide open, nothing but blackness on the other side. The darkness shifted around like wisps of dark mist.

Liz felt a tug on her arm and glanced over to see the boy, transfixedly treading toward the doors.

No! Stop! She tried to scream, but her mouth determinedly stayed shut, the words dying before they even reached her lips. The boy pulled at her arm insistently, and she reluctantly let go, letting him go freely toward his own fate as she turned to run. The black cloud shrouded the boy in darkness and, as Liz glanced over her shoulder, started to chase after her too. The loud shriek only grew louder, and the blackness caught up to Liz, pinning her limbs in place and going down her throat, suffocating her –

She gasped as her eyes opened to darkness. For a moment she was worried that she was still stuck in the strange black cloud that came from behind the doors. Then she saw the trees and the dark sky, the moon's light broken up by branches. Except the shriek didn't stop. Alarmed, Liz looked around to see Seth sitting up, urging them awake.

"We need to get out of here, now!" he barked, yanking both Liz and Liam up by their shoulders. The loud shriek was coming from the golden watchdog that Seth had cast earlier in the night, its mouth open wide in a low howl. Seth snapped his fingers at it, and it vanished.

They quickly mounted their horses, leaving most of their provisions behind. Liz and Liam were both on Liam's horse with Seth on his own to guide them. The horses had grown restless, pawing at the ground and snorting nervously. Almost as soon as they were ready to go, the horses set off without having to be told. Liz's injured horse severely limited their pace, even with Seth pulling it along. It was breathing heavily, its nostrils wide, still favoring its leg.

Soon they heard fast, light footsteps behind them. Liz was too scared to look over her shoulder at first, but she couldn't stand not knowing whatever was behind them.

Demons. Six or seven demons were streaking after them like shadows in the night, gracefully leaping over fallen trees and undergrowth. They were unnaturally tall, but their shapes were almost liquid-like as they twisted and turned around any obstacles in their path. They looked exactly like the one in Liz's dream, empty hollows for eyes and crooked smiles as they pursued their prey. Long claws reached almost to the ground as they smoothly glided over the forest floor.

With a regretful look, Seth released Liz's horse and pushed his heels into his own horse's sides. Without the injured horse, they could go at a full gallop, their only hope of outrunning the demons. Unfamiliar with the landscape, the horses were clumsier than the demons, who seemed to be slowed down by nothing.

The demons were gaining on them. They were difficult to see in the darkness of night, blending into the shadows. But the moonlight illuminated their slim shapes darting through the trees, and Liz couldn't tear her eyes away from them. Paralyzed by fear, she could feel her heart pounding, her palms warm and sweaty. It felt like the demons were staring at her, even without eyes.

Liz's old horse, no longer being pulled along, lagged behind. Its eyes were wide with panic as it clambered over branches and stumbled through bushes. Then a demon leveled with the horse and swiped toward it with a large clawed hand. Liz looked away and clamped her eyes shut as a loud scream issued from the horse. She heard a thump behind them and knew that it had fallen to the ground, already dead. The demons kept coming without hesitating.

Seth let his horse fall behind Liz and Liam by just an inch. He turned and a chain of lightning left his fingertips, striking one demon in the chest. It stumbled but didn't stop. As Liz watched, another bolt of lightning hit the same demon and it fell, its shadowy form falling apart before it vanished. But the rest were catching up too quickly. Seth couldn't possibly sto pthem all before they caught up.

Sharp pains were spiking through Liz's head. Her vision had black splotches all over. She was so disoriented that she could hardly even tell if she was looking ahead of them or behind, moving or not moving. Something wet was on her face – terrified tears. She felt sure that this was how she was going to die, torn apart by demons.

From far away, she heard Seth yell something. Liam screamed a response. Then he raised his hands and let out a powerful blast of fire, which covered the ground behind them. Poorly aimed and timed, it missed its target. The demons slinked around the patch of fire, which was devouring the dry foliage around it and spreading quickly, but they didn't slow down or stop. Liz whimpered and closed her eyes tightly, trying to shut out her fear and the pain inside her head.

Already terrified by the demons, the horses fled even faster with the growing fire behind them. It crackled and popped, but the sound was soon left behind. Looking back over her shoulder though, Liz could see it had already grown to show a steady blaze with no signs of stopping.

They'd covered quite some distance away from the fire. The demons, having slowly gained on them, were now only feet behind them, reaching out with their freakish claws. Letting out maniacal, triumphant laughter, their very presence chilled Liz's spine. She was hardly conscious by now, her fear shutting her entire brain off.

One demon menacingly growled, "Give us the girl!"

"Stay away from her!" Seth roared from their side, shooting another bolt of lightning from his hands. The explosion that resulted caused the demons to fly back, airborne, and Liam's horse to stumble to the ground before jumping back up and racing away, following Seth. But Liz had finally blacked out.

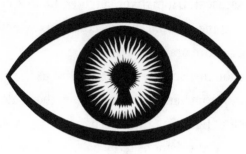

Chapter 4

WHEN LIZ CAME TO, SHE WAS LYING ON HER BACK in the dirt, a large bush over her greeting her open eyes. There were cuts where she'd fallen through the spiky plant, and scrapes where she must have tumbled on the ground. The air, she quickly realized, was thick with smoke. Her eyes were already watering. Somewhere, she could hear the popping and crackling of a fire but, disoriented, had no idea where it was coming from.

Through the smoke, she could see red streaks in the sky as the sun rose. Dazed and confused, she tried to sit up to get a better bearing of her surroundings. Not knowing what else to do, she tried to call out for Liam, but her throat was scratchy, and all that came out was a pained whimper. Another followed as the pain all hit at once. The soreness that had already been there from riding and sleeping on the hard ground, and now the aching from falling off of Liam's horse. She was half-convinced that she'd broken some bones, but nothing was apparently wrong.

A far-off voice caught her attention. She fought off her exhaustion to sit up and blearily search for the source. In her head, she was still trying to figure out if she'd died. Maybe they'd all died and gone to hell.

Liz was finally able to determine some of what the voice was saying. "I think it was around here somewhere..." She heard her name a few times, and it was getting closer. It was Liam's voice. She tried to shout out Liam's name to get his attention, but all she could manage was a painful cough. She couldn't stop blinking against the heavy smoke, and she felt like she was choking.

"She's over here!" she heard Liam call.

Liam and Seth appeared from behind some bushes, blinking rapidly with tear-filled eyes.

"Hurry," Seth panted, his voice sounding strained. He pulled Liz up by her shoulders. She almost fell over, her head pounding with the worst headache she'd ever had. She decided that she must have hit her head when she fell off of the horse. Being in the thick smoke wouldn't have helped at all.

Liz heavily leaned on Liam, Seth hovering behind them just in case, as they made their way back in the direction Seth and Liam had come from. Before long, the crackling of a growing fire disappeared, and the smoke began to dissipate as well. Liz's head started to feel clearer, and she'd regained her own balance enough to walk without Liam's support. Though she wasn't feeling as dazed, her head was still pounding from her fall to the forest floor.

After what seemed like an eternity, the smoke had become only a slight haze, and they were able to open their eyes wide enough to see again. Liz's throat felt choked up, and her lungs were still filled with smoke. It was difficult to breathe for the three of them, and occasionally one of them would give a great, hacking cough. At some point, Liz became aware that they weren't riding the horses, and she managed to ask where they'd gone.

"They got spooked and ran off," Seth answered. His voice sounded rough.

"What about the demons?" Liz questioned with a twinge of fear, looking over her shoulder. All she saw was a plume of smoke going upwards into the sky behind them.

Seth followed her gaze before answering. "The fire, or that explosion, I don't know – it spooked them too. They all ran off after a while." He cleared his throat.

Even after the smoke had cleared up, Liz's lungs felt heavy, and her eyes were puffy and red. All of her muscles were screaming at her to stop moving, her vision still swimming. But her fear kept her going, and she knew that they couldn't afford to stop. Not with the fire, and not with the demons on their trail.

"We're taking a break here," Seth announced with a glance behind them. They were in a huge field at the very base of the mountains, rolling hills separating them still from the massive Southern Peaks. Lit up beautifully by a full moon, the scene looked less intimidating than Liz figured it would look during the day. Trees dotted the surrounding landscape here and there, but the forest had ended.

However, looking behind them to the forest, Liz could see thick smoke clogging the sky in the distance. The fire was still raging, far away now. Hopefully it would keep the demons at bay for a while longer. But at the same time, Liz's heart sank. The fire marked where they'd been, leaving a clear indication of which way they'd fled from Koln for the demons to follow.

They were only a few days' march from Aloria now, even without the horses. The Southern Peaks ahead of them were just a small range separating the southwestern portion of the Alorian Peninsula from the rest of the continent.

Still, understandably, incredibly sore, Liz grimaced as she sat down on what looked like the softest patch of grass. They'd lost most of their provisions when the horses had fled. Now, Liz's stomach ached with hunger. To make her feel even worse, her clothes were filthy. She smelled strongly of sweat even though it had long since dried. Liam, in no better condition, joined her on the hard ground. His eyes were blank as he stared forward.

Neither of them said anything for a long while. Seth stood off to the side, intently watching the trees behind them. With a sudden feeling of weakness, Liz leaned against her brother's shoulder, trying to hold the tears off. But she couldn't stop the rapid thoughts and images going through her head. Everything had changed so quickly. She didn't know if she would ever see Alina again. Koln had been her home, and now it was probably burned to the ground. Soon enough, the tears were freely falling down, leaving clean tracks through the dirt packed on Liz's face.

Everything that had happened had been leading up to this moment. This moment, calm and quiet, during which Liz fell apart. Liz hadn't known it at the time, but that day the Prophet was trying to escape the Home had been the old woman's first attempt to talk to Liz. And then, eventually, the Prophet had told her that she was Chosen. Having no idea what that word was, what it meant for her, Liz had tried to brush it off. But now, the word echoed throughout her mind, over and over, only overlapped by one thing... The doors.

They're coming for you.

The sudden voice startled Liz. She glanced around, but neither Liam nor Seth had said the words, and it seemed like they hadn't heard them either.

"How's everything going over there?" Seth asked, catching Liz's eye as she searched for the source of the voice. Feeling unsure about telling him what she'd heard, Liz dumbly stared at him. Maybe it had just been her imagination...

Liam shrugged and stood up. He wandered over to Seth, and they began to speak in hushed voices. Liz, with an inward sigh, suspected that they were talking about her.

"... just tired..." she heard Liam saying. "... nightmares all the time... She's starting to see and hear things is all." With a feeling of anguish, Liz rested her chin on her knees and covered her face.

They were allowed to doze off after a while. As the sun began to rise, Seth roused them from their restless sleep. They began the long trek through the mountains.

The next day was uneventful. Exhausted and sore, Liz stumbled along behind Seth, Liam behind her. Despite Liz's inward aches and complaints, they only stopped twice throughout the entire day to get water at a small stream. Seth reminded her, when she asked if they could stop again, that they were out of food, and they had to get to Aloria as soon as possible if they didn't want to starve to death. She thought to herself that they might die of exhaustion instead if he kept dragging them along at this pace.

Liz was following Seth and Liam along a ridge that rose far above the surrounding area. Looking down, she saw that the cliff edge vanished in darkness on either side. The sky was orange, and there was no sun or moon. Farther off in the distance, other mountains peeked up above a layer of clouds. Vaguely, she was aware that none of this was real, but she still felt uncomfortable with the ledges only inches away from her feet. One wrong step and she'd fall to her death.

Seth and Liam seemed to be having a hearty debate, but Liz couldn't understand what they were saying. She glanced down at her feet, balancing on the thin crest of an unseen mountain. When she looked back up, Seth and Liam were farther ahead. Liz hurried after them, but they continued to get farther ahead until she could no longer even catch their voices on the wind.

Wait, she tried to call out, but her mouth refused to open. Rushing to catch up, she looked down at her feet again to see that the ground was crumbling beneath her. No-

For a moment, all she could see were two specks in the distance – Seth and Liam – on the mountain, and she was suspended in nothingness. Then she began to fall, letting out a silent scream.

The rest of the night passed similarly, her mind full of nightmares. But, thankfully, not the doors.

When Seth woke her a couple of hours before sunrise, she fought her muscles trying to stand up. She was so sore, she could barely feel her legs or her back at all.

They marched on, eventually stopping at a small creek gurgling its way across their path. Parched, Liz split off from Liam and Seth, kneeling down to the water. She pooled some in her hands and ungracefully splashed her face. She poured even more down her throat until she almost felt sick.

Clear, cool water flowed smoothly over colorful rocks. Red, gray, green, black...wait, she thought, narrowing her eyes suspiciously. The black wasn't from rocks at all, she realized, as she stared at the water. The black was on the surface, a shadow.

Transfixed, she watched as the shadow took a more solid, humanoid shape with no facial features. Then two slits opened up as eyes, pure red and malicious. A menacing grin formed below the eyes, making Liz's heart drop. She couldn't move, watching n horror as the shadow lifted itself up from the water and towered above her. The demon reached out an arm and hooked its long claws around her throat.

"Liz!"

Suddenly, she was on her back, staring at a cloudy sky. Liam was standing over her, Seth crouching beside them. He'd just splashed her face with cold water.

She sat up and frantically looked around for the demon, but it was nowhere to be seen.

"What – what happened?" she demanded, her heart still pounding so hard it hurt.

"You just kind of... fell over," Liam answered, sounding perplexed. "Are you okay?"

Liz looked at the spot where the demon had been. The water flowed peacefully over the rocks, no sign of the shadowy form.

"Yeah... I guess so," she said. "I thought I saw –" She hesitated for a moment. "I thought I saw a demon."

Seth was immediately alert, scanning the surrounding area with keen eyes. "Where?"

"In the water."

He looked hard at the water for a few moments with narrow eyes. "Well," he stated at last, "there's nothing there now."

"Were you just imagining it?" Liam asked, sounding worried. "I know you haven't been able to sleep lately..."

"I've been sleeping just fine," Liz snapped, trying to cover up her discomfort. Inwardly shuddering, she added, "But I must have just imagined it..." Forcing herself to raise her eyes, she looked up at Liam. "I'm fine."

Looking only slightly relieved, Liam nodded and offered a hand. Liz took it, and he pulled her to her feet. Seth still looked wary, but he relaxed a bit, and they continued across the stream. Looking over her shoulder, Liz thought she saw a small shadow flick through the trees on the other side, going back the way they'd come.

Chapter 5

THE SOUTHERN PEAKS ENDED ABRUPTLY WHEN LIZ wasn't paying attention, struggling to keep up with Seth's fast pace. One moment they were climbing up a steep hill, and then the next, they were faced by gentle hills that led to vast plains, tall grass shimmering in a light breeze. Liz felt weak from hunger and exhaustion, her whole body screaming at her to stop and give in to sweet, sweet sleep...

"Liz?"

Liz started at Liam's voice. Seth and Liam had walked a few paces ahead of her while she had stopped completely, eyes closed and body swaying.

"Yes, s-sorry," she stammered, stumbling forward to catch up to them. Her eyes caught sight of the area in front of them for the first time, and she stopped again, mouth slightly ajar. Her thoughts of giving way to sleep were overridden by her disbelief that they'd made it this far. Finally, they'd made it through the mountains, and with minimal trouble. Aloria wasn't far away.

They came to a small lake around sunset and camped at the edge of the water. Seth left to search for some food, as he'd seen some bushes in the distance that may have had edible berries growing on them. As he got farther away, the joyous feeling Liz had had from leaving the mountains was gone. Feeling empty again, she looked over the lake. Bathed in red light, it looked like it could've been a pool of blood. If she didn't feel so numb, she might have shivered in discomfort.

Seth eventually came back with his hands full of small, blue berries. Though they each didn't get very many, and the berries tasted sour, Liz's stomach groaned in appreciation at the small amount of food. When she finished her share, it continued to grumble, and a sharp pain came to rest there. She grimaced and tried to ignore it.

The sky had been clear when they'd first come to the lake. But as the sunlight faded, clouds crept into the sky, hiding the moon and stars. It was dark as a result, almost pitch-black. A clap of thunder sounded from far away, and the following bouts of thunder started to sound closer and closer by the minute.

"You might want to get some sleep before it rains," Seth suggested to them. "Once that starts, we might as well keep walking." Liz nodded, barely hearing him. As her eyes closed, she saw the golden outline of the dog appear again. Then all she saw was darkness.

Raindrops and a low growling woke Liz up. It was still dark, so she must have not been asleep for long. Looking around, she could hardly see anything past Seth. He was facing the way they'd come with a defensive stance.

"Show yourself!" he challenged, rousing Liam from his slumber. Feeling her blood run cold, suddenly wide awake, Liz looked past Seth to see the tall grass parting in a beeline straight for them. Something was coming. Liz quickly got to her feet, thinking that it could only be demons. They'd found her again.

A dark shape emerged from the grass, crawling on all fours. It had long claws protruding from its fingertips, making small but frightening clicking sounds on the ground. There were only red slits for eyes. A crooked, disturbing smile came onto its dark face as its eyes seemed to focus on Liz. Its shape was liquid-like, just like the other demons that had chased them before. Then it took a step forward, and five others appeared from the grass, advancing on Seth. Liz had a feeling that these were the same demons as the ones that had been in the forest. The wind rose up for a moment and brought forth a peculiar smell of ash.

"Get out of here!" Seth ordered to Liz and Liam. "Keep north!" There was a desperate note to his determined voice, but he didn't cower away from the group of demons. Liz didn't need him to tell her twice. She ran, Liam on her heels.

Thunder boomed above them, and the rain began to fall harder. Lightning flashed, blinding Liz for a few seconds.

She couldn't clearly see the ground, and didn't really care to try in her panic. Tripping on rocks and small dips, she soon hear ominous cackling behind her as the demons approached Seth. A crash sounded behind her, and she knew that Seth was throwing lightning at the demons.

Seth screamed in pain. And then the sound of pounding footsteps started to follow Liz and Liam.

Fueled by panic, Liz ran without knowing where she was going. All she knew was that she had to get away. Seth was likely dead. She had to get away. Without warning, her foot caught in a gopher hole. She cried out in pain, pulling her foot out and taking a stumbled pace forward. Liam grabbed her by the arm and shouted over the thunder, "Be careful!"

She'd twisted her ankle, limping terribly and lagging behind. Liam grabbed her by the arm again, forcing her to stop. His hands began to glow green as he reached for her foot. Liz almost fought to get away, but immediate relief flooded through her foot. For just a moment, she relaxed in the warm feeling, and then it vanished, and Liam was moving again, pulling her by the arm.

He'd only healed it for a couple of seconds, but it was enough for Liz to run. She couldn't hear the demons behind them, but she was sure they were quickly gaining on them both. Yanking her arm away from Liam, she sped past him, an unfamiliar feeling pulsing through her veins. Adrenaline, she realized somewhere in the back of her head. Right now, the word meant nothing to her. All that mattered was getting away from the demons.

Only seconds had passed – or maybe several minutes, Liz couldn't tell – when she and Liam saw a large group of dark shapes moving across the hills ahead of them. Heart leaping into her throat, Liz turned in a random direction, in a panic, and blindly ran.

A loose rock slipped under Liz's foot, and she fell to the ground with a startled gasp. A snarl behind her made her flip onto her back. One of the demons was looming over her, claws raised to attack. It growled again, and Liz screamed, showing her foot into the demon's chest as it swiped at her. Her face began to burn as blood dripped from fresh scratches on her cheek and forehead. The demon, recovering from her kick, reached up again for another hit.

A fireball slammed straight into the demon's face. It flew up into the air and over onto its back, squirming in agony. Liam appeared, helping Liz to her feet. She stumbled along behind him until she caught her balance again. Then she realized that they were running straight for the dark shapes she'd seen, which she, in her terror, only assumed were more demons.

Then one of the demons let out a shout that sounded strangely human. Between the furious thunderclaps, split apart by only seconds now, Liz could suddenly hear horses galloping toward them. Disoriented and confused, Liz turned her head this way and that, trying to find the source of the sounds in the dark. The "demons" were all around her now, and she realized that they weren't demons at all. They were humans on horseback.

Thunder and the sounds of battle were all around her now, and she became aware of a dim light up ahead. Just in front of her, an arm suddenly barred her way. Without thinking, she ran straight into it. Momentum kept her lower half moving forward while the rest of her was brought to a sharp stop, plummeting toward the ground. Bracing for impact, she was surprised when another arm effortlessly caught her, cupping her head in its hand with its elbow cradling her lower back.

The source of the light was a light spell, a small orb hovering behind the face now looking down at Liz. It was a young man's face, perhaps about twenty years old, with a neat beard and bright eyes. Without proper lighting, Liz couldn't tell what color the beard or his eyes were.

Bewildered, Liz barely understood him when he said, "It's okay." Realizing that she was no longer in danger, the rush within her stopped. She felt her heartbeat slow down, and her eyes began to close from exhaustion. Just before she lost consciousness, he added, "You're safe now."

When she awoke, she was in more pain than she'd ever been in in her life. All of her muscles seemed like they were on fire. Her ankle, while having been slightly healed by her brother, still ached. The scratches on her face burned like they were infected, which they probably were. Grimacing, Liz let out a small groan. Suddenly she realized that she was surrounded by soft voices. None of them answered her low moan of pain.

Sitting up, her face contorting for a moment as her muscles

screamed, she blearily looked around. Behind her, a group of people on horses rode in a disorganized bunch. A few of the horses drew wagons behind them, which had tarps covering whatever they carried. Liz was in the leading wagon with Liam lying next to her, a frown on his unconscious face. A young man was controlling the wagon. With a jolt, Liz recognized him as the man who'd caught her before she'd blacked out.

No one seemed to notice her, so she sat there uncertainly for a moment. Looking around in a daze, she jumped when she saw Seth in a wagon farther back. He looked like he was asleep – or dead – but as she watched, he stirred. Thankfully, he'd made it.

Looking back ahead, she cleared her throat, which ached, to try saying something. The man heard her and glanced at her over his shoulder, his eyes wide in surprise.

"Thank the gods," he murmured, then in a louder voice said, "You're alive. I was starting to wonder if I'd just imagined your pulse."

"No…" Liz said uncomfortably. Grateful as she was that these people had saved them from the demons, she worried now about what kind of people they were. "Um… Who are you?"

"You mean you don't know?" He sounded as surprised as he looked. "I'm Prince Thomas." Liz felt butterflies in her stomach flutter in embarrassment. Not that she would've had a reason to recognize him. She was suddenly nervous. Prince Thomas was the oldest of Queen Isabella's three children, and he was heir to the throne. He added, "But you can just call me Thomas."

A little taken aback by his casual attitude, Liz just stared at him wide-eyed. Her tongue was tied up in knots. He frowned and ordered the horse to stop, making her frightened that she'd done something wrong.

Turning to face the rest of the group, he announced in a loud voice, "We're taking a break here, everyone! Eat up." Then he looked back at Liz again, apparently concerned. "Are you okay? You look a little scared."

Liz blinked and tried to shrug off her mix of astonishment and discomfort. "Yeah, I'm just... What... What happened? Where are we?"

He seemed relieved that she was talking at least, and he calmly answered her. "We found you and your friends fighting against a horde of lesser demons. You two," he gestured to include Liam, "were running while the other man was trying to fight them off, I assume to protect you. We saw the demons and came to help, but then you all passed out." He directed his sharp gaze to Seth. "He almost died. He's been with our most experienced healer since we found him. He was all beat up, and he'll be sore for a while, to say the least. As for where we are, we're about a day's travel from Aloria. Now," he raised an eyebrow, "you should probably eat something. You've been out for a while. I just hope the others wake up soon. Hold on for a moment." He left, Liz's eyes following him as he made his way to one of the other wagons.

When he came back, a small-framed woman with long,

brown hair was following him. They carried some fresh fruit and bread, as well as a thermos that smelled strongly of hot chocolate, a beverage that had been considered a luxury in Koln.

"Thank you, Mira," Thomas said warmly, taking the food from her and setting it in the wagon next to Liz. Mira smiled and nodded before walking away. Thomas's eyes followed her for a few moments, then he turned to face Liz again. Interest gleamed in his bright eyes. "So let me guess – you're Chosen. That's why a member of the Royal Guard was protecting you with his life."

"Yes... I'm Chosen." The words felt strange leaving Liz's lips.

"May I ask your name?"

"I'm Elizabeth. Just... call me Liz though," she replied slowly, her eyes wandering to the unconscious Liam. "This is my brother, Liam. The... Royal Guard guy is Seth."

"Seth," Thomas repeated thoughtfully. "I'll have to give my mother a good report about him after all of this."

They didn't talk as Liz ate. Thomas wandered here and there, checking on the horses and the wagons, speaking with some of the other members of the expedition, always keeping an eye on Liz. Self-conscious and sore, she ate slowly and tried to make herself as small as possible. She could feel the eyes of some of the people on her, shining with curiosity.

When she got to the hot chocolate, Liz gulped it down greedily. She rarely got to taste such a beverage, as Alina had not been the most wealthy person. The thought of her mother made Liz's heart hurt, and she set the thermos back down, leaving a good portion of the food untouched. She hadn't eaten much, but her stomach already felt almost too full.

When she'd clearly finished, Thomas came back with Mira, playfully pushing her toward her wagon. She laughed as she lightly punched him in the shoulder in response. Smiling, Thomas looked back at Liz. "Are you ready to keep going? You might just want to sleep. I'm sure you're tired after what you've been through."

Liz just nodded, feeing too exhausted to speak. As they began to move again, she laid down in the wagon, staring at Liam's face. His chest rose and fell slowly, the frown still on his face. Bruises were scattered all along his body, on his face, his arms, his legs. In his slumber he shifted and groaned. Liz blinked once more, and, as uncomfortable as the wagon was, her exhaustion took her.

When Liz awoke, the first thing she heard was the light clattering of hooves on a stone path. Then she recognized Seth's voice, hoarse as it was.

"Are they both alive?" he was asking.

"Yes, thankfully," Thomas's voice answered him. "The boy is beaten up pretty badly, but the girl seems to be okay apart from those scratches on her face. Her ankle is swollen too. She was awake earlier."

She heard a sigh of relief from Seth, and a shadow fell across her face. Opening her eyes, she saw Seth looking back at her. He gave her a grim smile. "You okay?"

Liz groaned as she sat up. Though she'd slept through most of the day, she still felt exhausted and sore. "I'm... alive," she answered. Seth's face was covered in scratches, but they looked like they were already healing, probably thanks to a healing spell. His clothes were all torn up as well, but he seemed able to stand at least. For a moment Liz just sat there looking back at him, returning the small smile, and then the corners of her mouth twitched. Her face fell. Tears started dripping down, and she covered her eyes with her hands. "I was so scared," she whimpered.

Seth rested his hand on her shoulder and gently said, "You're safe now. We all are. We'll be in Aloria in a few hours, and nothing will hurt you there. We made it."

"What about Liam?" she asked desperately, looking back at her unconscious brother. "He hasn't woken up..."

"He's alive. We should be grateful for that much," Seth pointed out softly.

"I guess," Liz said bitterly, tearing her eyes away from Liam.

There were a few moments of uncomfortable silence before Thomas frowned and asked, "What happened that brought you three into that mess?"

"Well..." Seth started. "Demons came looking for Liz and Liam. We escaped Koln just in time, but the demons followed us back this way. They first caught up to us just south of the Southern Peaks, but we scared them off. Then they found us again, and that's when you showed up."

Thomas shifted uncomfortably. "How old are you and your brother?"

"I'm fifteen," Liz answered. "Liam's sixteen."

Pity flashed in Thomas's eyes, but only for a moment. He was about to say something when Seth continued, "Anyway, you won't have to do this without Liam. Look, he'll wake up soon."

Looking at her brother, Liz saw him twitch, and his unconscious face grimaced. Her own face was burning from the scratches the demon had inflicted. She reached up to tenderly touch them. There was one running along her forehead, one just below her eye, and another on her cheek. They felt like they'd scabbed over, but they still stung when she touched them. She quickly lowered her hand.

"Prince Thomas?" a woman's voice said from behind them. They all turned to see Mira approaching.

"What's up?" Thomas asked.

"I was just wondering if I should bring one of the healing experts to look at her scratches. They don't look like they'll heal instantly, but we can at least close them up a little."

"Sure, that would be great," Thomas said warmly. "Why don't you ride up here for a while?"

Mira blushed ever so slightly and glanced away. "I feel that it would be improper for someone like me to ride with the Prince." Her gaze hardened. "Especially because you're the Queen's heir."

"Don't mind that." It sounded as though they'd had this discussion before. "It's not her decision what I do with my life or who is in it."

"I can't," Mira said bitterly. "I'll bring one of the healers up here." She left at a brisk pace before Thomas could say anything else.

Seth watched her go and said quietly, "Pardon my saying, my Prince... But she will come around." Thomas narrowed his eyes at Seth, who met his gaze with an understanding look. "I've seen you two walking about the Palace grounds. It's no secret."

Thomas looked away, his eyes soft. "I don't want it to be a secret."

A moan from next to Liz took their attention away from Mira. Liam's eyes were barely open, but he was awake. Liz's mouth broke into an ecstatic smile. "Liam! Are you okay? Do you hurt?"

Liam's eyes opened a little more, and he looked over at her without moving his head. "What does it look like? Of course I hurt," he murmured slowly, his voice sounding strained. He closed his eyes tightly and grimaced. One of his eyes was swollen and purple. Liz watched him worriedly.

Another person rode up next to them and bowed to Thomas. "I'm here to heal some injuries."

"Fantastic," Thomas greeted him. "Liz has some scratches on her face, and Liam has a black eye as well as bruises everywhere. Perhaps start with Liz's scratches, and then move on to Liam. He will take a while longer than her."

Healing felt weird to Liz. She'd never needed someone to use a healing spell on her before. It caused her to itch as the healing process was sped up by the spell. At the same time, the scratches felt like cool water was pouring over them, sapping poison from her body. The healer moved on to Liam after a while, Liz reluctantly saying that the scratches indeed felt better. They couldn't heal them completely, but they no longer burned as though infected. Liam needed healing more than her, though she wished that Thomas had remembered her swollen ankle, which felt like pins were stuck in it.

After some time had passed, Liam was able to sit up. They brought him food, water, and a thermos with hot chocolate. Liz wasn't hungry so she skipped out on the food, but they'd brought her some hot chocolate too. She gulped it down without hesitation. After that, with the sun high in the sky, they kept moving.

Hours later, as the sun began to set, Liz yawned. Her legs itched to walk, but her ankle still tingled. "How much longer until we get there?" she asked Seth, who was still loyally treading beside them.

"Not much longer," he answered, stifling a yawn of his own. "See that group of trees over there?" He pointed out a small thicket of trees in the distance, alone in the midst of the great plains. Liz nodded, and he continued, "Those mean we're about half an hour away."

Liz looked back at her brother, who was still sleeping. As she watched, his face twitched, and he sat up. Looking around, he asked, "Where are we? Are we there yet?"

"Almost," Seth replied.

After what seemed like forever, listening to the indistinct murmur of the people around her, Liz saw something rising on the horizon. At first, she thought that it was another mountain range. But as they got closer, she realized that it was a wall. A huge, towering wall.

"Is that…" she trailed off, in awe already.

Seth smiled and nodded. "Aloria."

Chapter 6

LIZ AND LIAM WERE BOTH SPEECHLESS AS THEY APPROACHED the wall. It rose high into the air, a giant stone monument, for at least sixty feet. Beyond it, they could see the very top of a few buildings that must have been at least seven stories tall. It was unheard of to them, coming from an isolated village south of the Southern Peaks. There was a foul smell in the air that Liz had never smelled before. Turning to Seth, she asked what it was.

"That," Seth answered somewhat fondly, "is the smell of industry. Asphalt roads and cars, as well as factories."

Wrinkling her nose, Liz turned back to the city gates just as they began to open. Her mouth agape, Liz looked up as they passed through the gate. The stone above her was smooth, a dark gray. It went on for several feet as she imagined the weight of the stone wall above her. Then they were inside the city.

Unlike the buildings she'd seen towering higher than the wall, there were one-story barracks just inside the gate. Soldiers and guards were patrolling, looking grim. Behind them, Liz saw some of their own group scatter to different areas of the barracks, being dismissed from the expedition group. They looked solemn as well, quite different from Thomas, Seth, and the rest of the group remaining. They made their way farther into the city.

Stopping near a small booth, Seth beckoned to Liz and Liam to get out of the wagon at last. For a brief moment, Liz was relieved that they were finally getting to stand up and walk on their own feet. But as she scooted herself to the edge of the wagon, she was painfully reminded of the soreness in her limbs. Landing on the ground, her ankle twisted again, and she stumbled forward. Seth caught and steadied her as she grimaced.

"You okay?" he asked with a sympathetic look.

"I guess," Liz groaned.

When Liam got out of the wagon, his eyelids flickered as he started to fall. Mira, standing closest to him, caught him and awkwardly pushed him to his feet again. Liam leaned against the wagon, one hand on his forehead with his eyes closed tightly in pain.

"You'll need a healer and a good night's rest when we get to the Palace," Thomas commented, observing Liam. His eyes flicked to Liz, and he added, "Both of you." With that, he stepped into the nearby booth.

"What's in there?" Liz asked Seth, her face still tense with discomfort.

Seth followed her gaze. "That's a phone booth. Prince Thomas is calling for our ride back to the Palace." He gave Liz an amused look. "You didn't think we'd be riding all the way back in this wagon, did you?"

"All I've been thinking about is whether I'm going to die or not," she thought to herself.

Thomas came back out, an ecstatic smile on his face. "Ride's on the way," he announced. A few people cheered, the rest engaging in conversation with one another. Liz heard Seth start talking to Thomas in a quiet voice.

"Thank you for saving us. For saving them."

Thomas discreetly glanced at Liz and Liam. "I'm not sure if you should be thanking me."

Seth, looking confused, said, "But they'll be safe here. I mean, they're just kids. They've been in enough danger for now."

After a moment's hesitation, Thomas grinned. "You're right. It's a good thing I like to hunt in the Southern Peaks, otherwise we wouldn't have found you at all."

"They would have died," Seth murmured distantly. "Thank you again. I'm sorry we had to interrupt your trip."

"It was no problem," Thomas assured him. "Their safety is more important than my hunting."

The conversation stopped, and Liz, feeling as though she shouldn't have heard a word, quickly pretended to not have been paying attention. Observing the buildings around her, as Liam was doing, she was both surprised and confused to see their ramshackle appearance. Wilted flowers rose from aged window boxes, and old brick buildings looked ready to fall. The buildings were close together, all two stories tall. They looked very different from the taller buildings she could see in the distance. She wondered if the taller buildings also looked worse up close. Maybe this was what Aloria really was.

The acrid scent of "industry" was beginning to make Liz's head ache. Another putrid scent, of rotted food and urine, hit Liz's nose. At the same time, a knobby hand caught her shoulder. Letting out a yelp, she spun around, bumping into Liam. Together they looked at the man who stood before them.

He was an old man, his skin dark from his days under the sun. Through his torn and stained shirt, they could see his ribs sticking out from his skin. His hair was long and white, his facial hair ungroomed and dirty. His ancient eyes were sunken in, and his hopeful smile revealed that many of his teeth were missing. The ones remaining were very yellow, and his breath reeked of alcohol. He wore no shoes, and a toe poked out of the single sock he wore. Taking this all in at once, Liz opened her mouth in shock, but nothing came out.

The old man held out a small, silver can and mumbled something. Liz resisted the urge to recoil and instead said, "I–I'm sorry?"

He continued speaking, but Liz could only pick out two

words. "… spare change…"

She had no money, but she couldn't take her eyes away from his bedraggled appearance. Horrified and frightened, she felt intense relief when Seth stepped in, saying roughly, "They have nothing to give. Go back to where you came from."

The smile faded from the old man's face, and he hovered there for a moment as if not sure what to do. But when Seth turned away, cutting him off, he began to shamble away, limping slightly. He stumbled once and then disappeared between two buildings. Liz stared after him, pity in her eyes. She wanted to help him, though he'd scared her at first.

"Don't mind them," Seth reassured her. "You just have to know how to deal with them."

"Are there a lot of… them… around here?" Liam asked, sounding nervous. Seth looked after the man, his eyes narrow.

"Just around this part of the city. Once we get closer to the Palace, you won't be seeing any of them."

Before long, Liz heard a small rumbling noise somewhere nearby. As she tried to figure out what it was, a long car pulled up in front of them. She realized that this must be a limousine.

It was long, all white on the outside, a mix of black and white on the inside. White carpet and a black bench on one side, with the other side holding a small bar with all sorts of alcoholic beverages. Liz wasn't used to alcohol and felt a bit uncomfortable sitting across from it. She had no idea what any of it was called, and the mixtures other people were making smelled as bad as the "industry" smell Seth had mentioned. Alina had never kept alcohol in the house. But the bench felt more comfortable than anything she'd felt in days. It almost seemed to relieve her stiff muscles to sit down on a regular seat.

Once they were all inside – eight of them remaining from the hunting group – the limo set off, hitting some bumps on the unkept road. Liz stared out of the large windows, which gave her a clear view of the lower district of Aloria. The capital she'd heard so much about wasn't what she saw here.

Inside the limo was a bunch of happy chatter as drinks and food were shared. But outside of the limo, an entirely different scene greeted Liz's eyes. The asphalt road had limitless potholes, and the road was narrow. Liz had heard that everyone in the capital of Alyspar had cars, but no cars parked on the curb here. The houses were small and rundown, looking like they were about to fall apart.

"Do people... live out here?" Liz asked Seth, who was sitting next to her.

"Yes," he responded, sounding surprised as he followed her gaze out the window. "There are houses, aren't there?"

"It looks worse than Koln," she commented quietly.

"This is the lower district," Seth informed her in response. "Most of these people don't have jobs, and they haven't ever gotten an education. This is what they can afford." He didn't sound remorseful or sympathetic. Liz blinked as the small houses and buildings passed by. She felt like she'd been slapped by their very appearance. It wasn't at all as she'd expected.

There was a woman, her hair messy and dirty, clothes torn and worn out, sitting outside of an old house. She was smoking a cigarette. She watched the limo drive by with an empty look in her eyes, flicked the cigarette to the ground, and made her way through a broken screen door into the house.

Many of the houses had broken doors and boarded up windows. Trash was scattered all about almost every lawn. Any grass – for most of the ground was just dirt – was yellow-brown and dead. There were no street lamps or sidewalks. Liz took all of this in as the limo continued to bounce over potholes and bumps in the road.

She caught sight of a small group of children standing around a dumpster. As she watched, one child appeared and jumped out of the dumpster, holding a small box of old food. Triumphant, they ran away down the alleyway, and Liz couldn't see them any longer. This definitely wasn't the grand capital city she'd read about, where everyone was safe and happy. These people were suffering.

"To Alyspar!" a sudden shout made her jump. Thomas, with a sly smile, passed a cup of wine to Mira beside him and then spread glasses around until everyone – excluding Liz, Liam, and Seth, who refused to take a drink while still on duty – had a glass of red wine. They all took a sip, celebrating their country... while Liz doubted more than she ever had that Alyspar was a fair place, where everyone had an equal chance at a good life.

As if to prove her thoughts, they passed a stretch of road where several people, looking extremely unkempt, were standing outside. Many of them glared at the limo as it passed, and some of them threw things. Liz flinched as a brown banana peel hit the window. No one seemed to care or even notice.

"Why do they do that?" she asked.

Liam added, "Shouldn't they be happy that we're here to help? As Chosen, I mean."

"Unfortunately, most of them blame the royal family for their problems. They know that the Prince is in here, and it makes them upset," Seth explained with an irritated roll of his eyes. "You'd think they would show him proper respect. They're lucky he's been drinking. Usually, he doesn't allow them to disrespect him, and thus this country, this much."

Liz watched the houses go by, old buildings that were cramped and now more often two stories high. They looked like they were apartments now, rather than houses, though they were still falling apart. She wondered if it really could be the people's fault if they lived here, or if it was their fault that this was all they could afford. Having lived in Koln for the entirety of her life, she felt very detached from the apparent divisions between people in the capital. She wondered where she would have been if she was living here.

Outside, a little boy stood in one of the dead yards, a small stick in his hand. A black dog wagged its tail at his smiling face, and the boy threw the stick. The dog chased after it and took it back to the boy, and then the limo had passed them. Liz was slightly relieved to see that at least someone here seemed happy. However, she still wasn't sure how to feel about the state of things in the lower district.

Eventually, they left the southern part of Aloria behind. The houses here were larger and more separated, sometimes with fences between them. Some yards were uncared for and yellow, but many of them were green with life. A few cars lined the streets, and sidewalks wound alongside the road. The road was clean, lacking potholes and bumps. They passed a group of children, who were crowded in one yard. Unlike the children by the dumpster Liz had seen earlier, these children wore clothes that looked aged but fit well enough, with no holes or stains. Just as the limo went around a corner, the children ran off in separate directions, playing some game.

"Are we still in the lower district?" Liz asked uncertainly.

"We're in the southcentral area now. It's part of the middle district," Seth informed her. "We're not far from the business district and downtown."

Liz glanced back the way they'd come, wondering why the poor people in the lower district weren't provided with better roads or housing. Certainly there was something the Queen could do about it. She was the Queen, after all. And just as baffling to Liz as this, it also seemed like no one else in the limo cared.

Distracted by her thoughts of social classes – a concept unfamiliar to her – Liz hadn't noticed the buildings getting taller. Before she knew it, they were six stories or more, covered in flashing lights that attracted her gaze. There was an electric sign that read "The Drunken Boar". The letters lit up one by one until the whole sign was lit up. Then it would flash twice and spell out the words again. Mesmerized, Liz watched it over and over with awe. She'd never seen an electric sign before. A few young people stumbled from the bar. One of the men carelessly slung an arm around one of the women's shoulders and whispered something in her ear. She burst into laughter that Liz could hear from inside the limo.

Steadily, more lights and signs brightened the sides of the buildings, saying things such as "The Starving Sasquatch" or "Maddie's", which looked to be a huge clothing store with multiple stories. They stopped suddenly, Liz lurching forward. Liz craned her neck to see lights hanging over the road. A bright red one was lit up. Traffic lights. The light turned green and, before they even began to move again, a loud horn sounded from behind them. Startled, Liz looked back, but she couldn't tell who had honked.

Traffic lights were at every intersection, causing them to stop often, giving Liz a clear view of downtown Aloria. Countless people were walking everywhere, crowding the sidewalks. Cars were lined up bumper to bumper along the road, both ahead of them and behind. Electric signs lit up the sides of most buildings now – banks, bars, restaurants, assorted shops. None of the buildings looked like houses anymore. Thye looked more like large blocks towering above them with windows spread evenly across every side. A large screen ahead of them showed a soda can dancing across the screen, advertising a local food joint.

The sound of people chattering, cars moving and honking,

bright signs surrounding them, and the people within the limo were all overwhelming Liz. She had a pounding headache, her eyes hurt, and the smell of this industrial city was too much for her sensitive nose. She hadn't been paying attention to the people surrounding her in the limo, but she now saw that they'd all become quite drunk. They sloshed wine around in their glasses and poured themselves more. The white carpet had red stains in it now all along the floor.

Smiling at Mira, Thomas tried to pour himself more wine. Instead, he missed his cup entirely and spilled it all over his own feet. He looked down with a curse. Mira giggled loudly.

"Driver," she hiccupped, "you need to replace the carpet again!" In the front of hte limo, the driver's shoulders rose and fell as though he'd sighed.

Nearby chanting attracted Liz's attention now, and she looked at a corner of the intersection they'd stopped at. On the street corner, a small group of people stood holding signs. One of the people turned, allowing Liz to read what the sign said: *Demons are people too!*

Liz, eyes trained on the signs, asked uncomfortably, "Who are they?"

Seth glowered at the group of people disdainfully. "Demons' rights activists. They think that demons are like people, feelings and all. They think we should treat demons the same way we treat other human beings, like they're just misunderstood."

With a glance at Liam – he was asleep by now, not paying attention to what was going on around them – Liz persisted,

"Why?"

"Who knows." Seth rolled his eyes. "They've never seen a demon before in their lives. They have no idea what demons have done to us. Our only option is to fight them, or else we'll be wiped out." After watching him for a moment with wide eyes, Liz looked back outside. The traffic light turned green, and they left the activists behind.

It was getting dark outside, the moon just a sliver shining in the fading purple sky. The bright signs were hurting Liz's eyes as they continued to flash and change. She blinked every couple seconds but couldn't bear to look away from everything around them. It was nothing like Koln – the tall buildings, the lights, the people. People wore all sorts of clothes with all sorts of hairstyles. Some of them, to Liz, looked ridiculous, but the people carried their heads high.

Another group of people was standing on the sidewalk with signs, and Liz thought for a second that they were more demons' rights activists. Instead, as the limo approached them, she saw that they wore tattered clothes, and their signs weren't about demons. These were people from the lower district, protesting the treatment of the poor.

Faintly, Liz could hear them shouting in unison: "A! B! C! Awareness of broken class systems! A! B! C!"

A person in the group made themselves heard over the others, staring daggers at the limo. "Your class system is why we suffer! You punish us for nothing we've done! We demand justice!"

They passed by the hostile group of people. As they

continued through downtown, Liz gradually became more and more aware of people lining the streets, looking much like the homeless man that had stopped her, back at the wall. They sat on the paved sidewalks with empty eyes. Some of them held out cans or bowls to passers-by, but to no avail. Most people seemed to just ignore them, stalking by without a second glance. Every once in a while, Liz would see one lying on the ground facing the wall of a building. She glanced around at the happy people in the limo. They didn't seem to care whatsoever about the poor people barely holding on to life on the streets.

Still feeling confused, she didn't realize that they'd left downtown behind until the sky was darker and more houses surrounded them. These houses were two or three stories high, each complete with high, arched entryways and huge windows compared to the houses they'd seen in the lower and middle districts. Streetlights lit up large, green yards and a wide road with cars parked alongside the curbs. Cars were also parked in individual driveways, oftentimes with more than one car. These cars, unlike the few ones in the middle district, were sleek and sporty, shiny even in the dim light from the streetlights.

"Is this the upper district?" Liz asked, holding back a yawn. She hadn't realized just how tired she was.

Seth nodded, the bags under his eyes apparent by now. "We're close to the Palace now. You might even be able to see it from here." He and Liz leaned a bit to the side, looking for the Palace up ahead.

A dome-shaped glass silhouette rose from behind another set of walls. These walls were not as tall as the walls surrounding the city, but they divided the Palace grounds from the outside. The glass dome looked gorgeous, like a pearl shining in a sea of brown. In awe, Liz's eyes grew wide.

"Is that the Palace?"

"Yes," Seth answered, looking relieved as he put his head back and closed his eyes.

The sky was nearly black now with a few stars shining up above. The eastern portion of the city was still lit up by the lights from downtown, but those lights were now far away as they approached the grand Palace.

At last, they were going through another set of gates that let them into the Palace grounds. It was too dark to see very much inside, but rolling hills and grassy fields stretched far off to the walls in every direction. The road to the Palace proper was long, but eventually they pulled up to the tall, glass dome. Seth stood up as the limo pulled to a stop, stretching his arms into the air. "We're here."

Chapter 7

SOFT, WHITE LIGHTS STRETCHED UP THE PATHWAY FROM the circular driveway to the doors of the Palace. The doors were pure white with brass handles, at least fifteen feet tall. It took three people on each side to open them. Thomas stood and stretched within the limo, declaring, "Home sweet home!" He grabbed Mira by the hand and lifted her up, dragging her out of the limo with him. Seth gazed after the Prince with an unreadable look before carefully prodding Liam. Liam's eyes opened wide as he jumped awake. For a moment he looked to be in a panic, but then when he gathered their surroundings, he relaxed.

"Are we there?" he asked sleepily.

"We are," Seth answered.

Liz's stomach growled as they exited the limo. Just like every other part of her body, her stomach ached. Part of her wanted to gorge herself with food, but another part of her just wanted to curl up and sleep. Now that she felt safe, she felt like maybe she would be able to get a good night's rest for the first time in days.

Many people greeted the hunting party on their arrival. Some of the people spoke to Seth quietly, glancing back at Liz and Liam with wonder in their eyes. Liz heard one of them ask, "They're really Chosen?" Then her line of sight was cut off by a boy who looked no older than eighteen. He was wearing fine clothes, his hazel eyes shimmering. His dirty blond hair was messy, almost as though he'd been running his hands through it all day.

"My name is Graham," he announced. "I'm training to be a Royal Guard and have been assigned to show you to the Feast Hall." Liz was leaning slightly to keep an eye on Seth, whom she didn't want to lose sight of. He had protected them and kept them safe. She trusted him, and until she was certain that she would be okay without him, she didn't want to leave his side.

Liam on the other hand had his eyes trained on Graham with interest. "There's food?"

Graham answered, "Absolutely. There's a feast tonight to celebrate Princess Arabella's sixteenth birthday." Catching onto Liz's inattention, he glanced over his shoulder at Seth, then gave her a grim smile. "I'm afraid he, as a fully fledged Royal Guard, has matters to attend to now that he's back. I know I'm no replacement, but I'll do my best. You're safe here."

They caught up to Seth as they walked down a spacious hallway. The floor was a soft white with perfectly spaced red carpets. Paintings coated the pure white walls: portraits of people, past Kings and Queens of Alyspar; breathtaking scenery, including mountains, lakes, and hillsides covered with flowers; paintings depicting the history of Alyspar, such as the establishment of Aloria and the defeat of greater demons, their names specified in plaques. The only name Liz managed to read, walking at their brisk pace, was Synder.

The greater demon looked huge compared to the Chosen facing it. However, Synder was letting out a screech of pain, the Chosen shooting bolts of darkness at it. Even as Liz imagined the scene in her head, the demon was evaporating into nothingness. Then they'd passed the painting, and Liz yawned, no longer able to keep up with the countless names on the walls.

Seth caught sight of them as they came upon another hallway splitting off in a different direction. At Liz and Liam's trusting gazes, waiting for him to tell them what to do, he gave them a sympathetic look. "I'd love to eat to my heart's content," he told them, "but I'm exhausted. I haven't slept properly in days. Hopefully I'll see you two around though," he added quickly at their crestfallen faces. "If I don't... it was nice meeting both of you. Good luck."

He reached out to shake Liam's hand. When he offered his hand to Liz as well, she dumbly stood there, staring at him in disbelief. A sudden wave of anxiousness washed over her at the thought of him leaving them after all that they'd been through in the last several days.

"Hey now," he said sternly when the silence had stretched longer. "Graham will take care of you from now on. He's my apprentice. I promise that you'll be safe with him."

At his comforting words, Liz felt her eyes tearing up. Ignoring his outstretched hand, she jumped forward to give him a hug. "Thank you for everything," she whispered. He hesitated for a moment, surprised, and then returned her hug.

"I'll keep an eye on them," Graham promised with a respectful nod to Seth. Seth gave him a grateful look. Liz detached herself from him and watched as he departed, alone, down the hall.

"The Feast Hall is right up here," Graham's words broke Liz out of her stupor. Liz could faintly hear voices from down the hallway that got louder and louder as they approached. Classical music was playing in the background, and the aroma of various foods suddenly hit Liz's nose. Her mouth watered, and her stomach growled in anticipation, having not eaten a proper meal in days. They rounded the corner to the Feast Hall. Liz's jaw dropped in awe.

Just through a tall, elegantly arched doorway was a room that seemed to stretch for miles with three long, wooden tables that ran the length of the room. At the other end of the room, another table reached from wall to wall so the people sitting there were facing Liz. Each table was crowded with people, all wearing fancy suits or dresses, looking flawless and beautiful. Liz felt inadequate suddenly in her torn clothes and with her dirty, tear-stianed face. The smell of food wafted to her nose though, and she focused on the idea of eating instead.

There were all kinds of foods, from pork chops to rice to fruit salad, from chicken legs to bread to corn. Large turkeys were scattered around each of the tables, along with mashed potatoes and even tofu. Drinks of all types, alcoholic and non-alcoholic, covered every spare inch of the table that wasn't already hidden by food. Juices, beers, wines, sodas, and waters were amongst the mixture of drinks.

Huge, intricate chandeliers hung from the ceiling, lighting up the entire space. They looked like they were made of glass. A wide archway separated this room from a side room, where the classical music was coming from. People moved to the music, laughing and dancing.

As Graham walked them toward the other end of the room, Liz suddenly felt nervous, a weight seeming to settle in her stomach. She could see Thomas sitting at the end table, but he'd passed out with his face flat on the table, probably from his consumption of so much alcohol. Next to him sat a boy who looked like he couldn't be any older than Liz. The boy's eyes were trained on them with great interest. Anxious, Liz looked over at Graham, who somehow seemed perfectly at ease.

"Are there always so many people?"

"Sure are," Graham answered cheerfully. "Her Majesty invites everyone in the Palace to the feasts, as well as some folks from the upper district. Some people come from other countries to answer her summons. This feast is especially important too – it's Arabella's birthday." Liz followed his fond gaze to a young girl sitting at the end table on the other side of Thomas. Her long, brown hair was twisted up in a high ponytail. They were now close enough for Liz to see Arabella's bright, hazel eyes. She was watching them with those hazel eyes, just like the boy, who Liz could only assume was Queen Isabella's youngest child, Prince Henry.

Next to Arabella, in the middle of the table, sat an older woman. Her hair, which looked to be a vibrant red, was curled up in a spiral on top of her head with a small braid encircling it. She was paying no attention to them, rather observing the people dancing in the side room with her head held high. At her side was a man, who Liz figured must be the King. Not a man of much ambition, he was content to sit back and let Queen Isabella do the ruling. She had been the one born into the royal family, after all.

"The Queen likes to meet all Chosen when they first enter the Palace," Graham explained. "It shouldn't take long, and then you can eat. She'll probably speak with you more in detail tomorrow."

Butterflies were swarming in Liz's stomach, making her nauseous. Her mouth was dry, and she couldn't make herself swallow. Palms sweaty at her sides, she desperately hoped that the Queen wouldn't want to shake her hand.

As the Queen caught sight of them, she stood. She was taller than both Liz and Liam by several inches. Graham, who towered above both Liz and Liam, was only an inch or two taller than her. He bowed low when Queen Isabella got close to them. Liz and Liam exchanged a glance and hastily bowed too.

"Milady," Graham said reverently, "I present to you the latest Chosen."

With a penetrating, harsh gaze, she appraised the two of them.

Finally, she spoke. "Who is this one?" She had her cold eyes pinned on Liam.

They all stayed silent, unsure of what to say. Even Graham blinked in confusion.

"Who are you?" Queen Isabella insisted, sounding annoyed now. "I called for an Elizabeth…" She gaze Liz a hard look. "But I don't remember anything about a… whoever you are."

Liz and Liam dumbly looked at Graham, not sure of what to say. He looked equally in shock, his mouth agape. He quickly closed it, swallowed, and seemingly found the courage to speak. "This is Elizabeth's brother, Liam. He… Isn't he Chosen?"

A spark of interest came and went in the Queen's eyes before she spoke again, snapping, "Well, I certainly did not ask for him." At their stricken faces, she gave a heavy sigh and passed a glare at all three of them in turn. "Fine. You may stay until tomorrow morning, but I can't guarantee that you'll be allowed to stay longer than that. I'll make my mind up tonight. Thank you, Graham. I'll trust you to lead them to their quarters for tonight after they've eaten."

With those sharp words, the Queen elegantly walked away. Even in her anger, she had an air of grace about her. It was obvious that she'd never known anything but a life of royalty.

For a weighted moment, they were all silent. Then Graham cleared his throat awkwardly. "Well, I guess you two had better eat, and then...we'll see what happens. She changes her mind often," he added hastily at the shocked Liam. Graham went on, "In the morning, I'll have one of the older guards talk to her. She'll probably calm down and let you stay. For now... I don't know about you guys, but I'm starving."

Liz's stomach had knotted up while talking to the Queen. Now, her appetite returned as soon as they sat down. She ravenously ate her fill, her meal consisting largely of desserts that had been considered a luxury back home. However, Liam simply moved the peas on his plate around with his spoon. His eyes were empty.

Later, long after midnight, Graham led a dejected and confused Liz and Liam to their separate rooms, dropping Liam off first. Her mind blank from exhaustion, Liz hardly noticed when Graham stopped and opened a door for her. Slipping through the door and closing it behind her, she barely saw the room except for the bed. She laid down, and within seconds, she'd fallen into an unfitful sleep.

Chapter 8

IN HER DREAMS, SHE SAW THE DEMONS AGAIN. THEY CHASED after her on all fours, their red eyes glittering with malice. With claws slicing the ground beneath them, they reached for Liz, just on her heels. She ran as fast as she could, but they came closer and closer until they reached her and –

She shot up in bed, breathing heavily. Her sheets were drenched with cold sweat, beads of it dripping down her face. Her heart was pounding much too fast, hurting her chest. Realizing that it had been a dream, she blinked and tried to relax. She'd had so many nightmares before that she was used to this. Somehow though, she had thought she'd be safe once she got to the Palace. But now, she realized, even though the demons couldn't get her physically, the walls didn't protect her from her nightmares. Overwhelmed by a sudden feeling of hopelessness, Liz covered her face with her hands and let out a quiet sob.

After a while, as exhaustion began to take her again, she was able to stop crying. The night prior, she had been too tired to give her room a proper look. It was quite bright, with large windows covered by thin curtains. The windows looked out over the Palace grounds facing the rest of Aloria. The business district loomed in the distance, buildings half-lit by a rising sun. Liz, still tired and glum, didn't take much time to admire the view. It had been overwhelming the night before, and she still yearned for the open space around Koln.

The bed was huge, larger than any bed Liz had ever slept on before. It was in a small nook in the room, surrounded by fully-stocked bookshelves. A variety of topics was covered by the books: everything from history to science to magic. On the wall opposite the bed was an ornate electric fireplace with a couple of large chairs beside it. The fireplace was on, giving the room a nice, warm temperature. A sliding door appeared to lead to a spacious private bathroom.

The first thing Liz noticed was the sleek look of the shower. It was a pearly white, a large step-in shower with a waterfall showerhead. The showerhead had different settings, which was something Liz had never seen in Koln. It was removable, allowing the directing of water whatever which way. Full bottles of shampoo, conditioner, body wash, and face wash were neatly organized on the side shelves. Shea sugar scrubs and other assorted things – Liz didn't even know what they were used for – took up the rest of the space. The second thing she noticed was the sizeable mirror on the wall… as well as her own appearance in it.

She hadn't been able to care about her hygeine for days now, being on the road and on the run. Her hair, unbrushed and unkempt, was greasy and sticking up in random places. There were clear lines where tears had fallen in her face, tracing patterns in the dirt that had built up. The scratches left by the demon just a few days before were clearly scored across one eyebrow and on her cheek. As if her body had forgotten about the scratches until now, they began to burn again as if they were fresh. Her shirt had a hole on the shoulder, revealing a large scrape. It was red and puffy, much like the scratches, showing signs of infection.

After staring for several moments at the reflection that she no longer recognized as herself, Liz searched the drawers in a shocked daze. Unable to comprehend most of what she saw, she managed to find toothpaste, a toothbrush, and a hairbrush. Once she'd cleaned herself up a bit - struggling with her hair for a good chunk of time - she stepped into the shower.

The warm water washed away her stress for a while, though her cuts and scrapes still burned as they came into contact with the water. Then unbidden memories of the night before - when the Queen had told them that Liam might have to leave the Palace - suddenly came to the forefront of her mind. Feeling nauseous, as though she'd been punched in the gut by an invisible enemy, Liz frantically got dressed and left her room.

The hallway stretched far away in both directions, different hallways branching off of it. They curved around the edge of the glass dome that was the Palace, the ends of the hallways wrapping out of sight. Having been too tired to keep track of where they'd come from the night before, Liz looked first in one direction and then the other, feeling at a loss. The silence felt heavy, making shivers run down her spine.

"Need help finding the Dining Hall?" a voice said, making Liz jump. She turned to see a Royal Guard standing outside of her door, where she hadn't noticed her at first. The woman seemed friendly enough.

"I need to find my brother, Liam," Liz said quietly.

"The first place he'll go is the Dining Hall. They told me you'd want to see him. Graham will be with him." The Royal Guard smiled and began to lead the way to the Dining Hall, hallway after hallway. Every hallway looked just like the last, until soon enough Liz felt so turned around that she was completely lost again. The Palace seemed even larger on the inside than it had on the outside, though it had towered over Liz the night before as much as every one of the buildings downtown.

The Dining Hall was smaller than the Feast Hall they'd eaten in the night prior. Small, glass tables were scattered throughout the room, and a large breakfast bar with a wide assortment of breakfast foods was against the entirety of the walls. People wandered freely past Liz and the guard out to the hallway, dispersing to their various duties. Liz looked around uncertainly at the tables until her eyes came to rest on Liam, who was sitting next to Graham at one of the tables.

Thanking the guard who'd escorted her, she hurried over to them.

Seeming to have been in a deep conversation, Liam and Graham grew silent as Liz approached. Liam wore an unreadable expression and, when she was within earshot, yawned, "There you are. We've been waiting all morning..." He didn't look nearly as hopeless as he'd been the night before. Liz gave them both a careful look, wondering if they'd heard about the Queen's decision.

"So we have some good news," Graham finally announced. "The Queen sent a messenger earlier to say that Liam can stay. I figure she was just upset last night because Prince Thomas showed up drunk again. I told you guys," he added, his relief evident in his tone.

Liz sighed and closed her eyes for a moment, the knots in her stomach loosening. Now that she knew her brother wasn't being sent away, she felt the illusion of safety and comfort come over her. For the first time since the Prophet had confronted her, she tried to embrace those feelings, not quite wanting to admit to herself the danger she would face as one of the Chosen. Eventually, she knew that she would have to complete the training necessary to fight the greater demon Xanedur. But for now, she let out her tense muscles and forced a smile onto her face.

"As a Royal Guard in training, I've been assigned to escort you two around the Palace for the day. So you don't get lost," Graham added when Liz and Liam exchanged a glance. "Seth would have done it, but he had some other matters to–" With a sudden smile, Graham cut himself off. "Well, well, look who we have here."

Princess Arabella had entered the room, head held high. Her hair was loose, flowing over her shoulders as she strode into sight. Graham's eyes caught hers. As she approached them, he explained, "Arabella and I go way back." Liz's eyes were wide, and she suddenly found it hard to swallow. The Princess looked nice enough, but she was still the daughter of the Queen, who had been so short with them before. Liz wondered if Arabella would be just as harsh and blunt.

At Graham's questioning look, Arabella grinned. "Archery practice. That's why I'm late." She turned her friendly eyes to Liz and Liam. "Let me guess – you two are the newest Chosen?" Liz looked down, uncomfortably remembering Queen Isabella implication that Liam wasn't Chosen. Liam was still, his expression unreadable.

Graham answered for them, "Elizabeth here is, but Liam… There was some sort of mistake."

Arabella frowned, giving Liam a concerned look. "Is my mother letting you stay anyway?" Liam glanced up with guarded eyes, obviously not sure if he should trust the Princess. Arabella added, "Don't worry. I'm not like my mother. I know how she gets. You can talk to me."

Looking away, Liam muttered, "She's letting me stay. For now." His voice sounded bitter. Liz cast him a worried glance, but he didn't look back at her.

Ignoring his reluctance to speak, Arabella flashed a mischievous smile. "Well, allow me to show you around on your first day. Most of the Chosen are older than us, so it's nice to have some our own age for once. There are a lot of secret places around the Palace that even my mother doesn't know about."

After they'd finished eating, they followed Arabella and Graham out into the hallway. Arabella and Graham play-fully poked fun at each other and laughed. Liz tried to share a carefully amused look with Liam, but her brother still seemed to be in a sour mood and didn't return her glance. A little stung, Liz tried to focus on the Princess and Graham instead. Despite Liam's reluctance to socialize, Liz could feel the butterflies in her stomach, which had been there for days now, were finally starting to fade away. It was easy to be around Arabella and Graham, with the relaxed atmosphere surrounding them like a bubble. Arabella was nothing like Queen Isabella had been the night before; she was easy to talk to, and she treated her royal blood so nonchalantly that it almost seemed like she was as normal as Graham.

From the way they were talking, Arabella took her ar-chery very seriously. Though guns were a lot more popular, she loved the feeling of a bow in her hand and a quiver of arrows on her back. Their conversation came to a sudden halt as Queen Isabella herself came around the hallway in front of them. Her sharp eyes grazed over them, lingering for a moment on Liam. The relaxed bubble surrounding them popped, replaced by a feeling of unease. They'd almost walked past her when she turned and called, "Bella, come here." Arabella winced but obliged.

Speaking in low voices, Queen Isabella and Arabella stared each other down. The Queen said something that must have upset Arabella because Arabella drew herself up to her full height, crossing her arms and shaking her head stubbornly. Finally the Queen exclaimed, "You'll do as you're told!" With that, she was walking away. Arabella rejoined them, looking furious.

"Bella?" Graham repeated in an attempt to diffuse the tension, smiling uncomfortably. "Nice."

"Shut up."

They resumed walking down the long, curved hallway until they reached an enormous room that stretched up for several floors, each floor with a balcony overlooking the area. A huge, beautiful, glass chandelier hung on a long chain decorated with smaller lights from the ceiling, though the light was unnecessary in broad daylight. Already in awe, Liz's jaw dropped when she looked to the side opposite the balconies. The wall was entirely made of glass. A small grass lawn turned into sand and then –

The ocean.

Aloria was on the shore of a large bay. Water stretched as far as the eye could see. A little ways down the beach, Liz could see piers reaching out over the water. In either direction, the distant wall surrounding the city could be seen. Liz's eyes gravitated toward the large expanse of water, bright and blue. The sky was so clear, she could hardly tell where the water ended and the sky began.

"People travel here from all over the world to visit my

mother," Arabella told them. She seemed much calmer now than when she'd been talking to the Queen. "Thun, Ghanz, Cujan... Anyone from anywhere who wants to see her."

"In other words, no one," Graham muttered with a small smirk. Liz was surprised to hear him insult the Queen, but Arabella just shrugged and smiled at Graham.

"You know that plenty of people come here for my mom's feasts. Just last night there were some people from Anar and Thun," she reminded him. Looking back out over the water, she added, "She may be... a pain, but she knows how to throw a party. Though I'm not sure why anyone cares anymore. Cujan doesn't even send people over anymore even though they're just north of us."

"Why is that?" Liz ventured to ask.

Arabella answered carefully, "Well... Let's just say they have some issues with how my mother does things."

Unsure of what she meant, Liz opened her mouth to ask which issues she could be referring to. But before the words escaped her lips, Liam suddenly turned to them. "Where to next?" His voice was unusually sharp. Liz studied him for a moment, as he'd been short-tempered all morning. Then he grazed his eyes over her. Quickly looking down and shuffling her feet, Liz decided that she was probably misreading him.

Arabella pondered for a moment. "There's the movie theater, if you want to check that out."

Neither Liz nor Liam had seen a movie theater before, and the idea of having one so accessible seemed unreal to them. Of course they wanted to see it.

They explored various parts of the Palace, poking their heads into abandoned rooms and admiring the view from balconies. The entire West Wing was reserved for guest rooms, and the East Wing was where the servants lived. The Upper Wing – the top floor – was where Arabella's room was, along with her brothers' and mother's rooms.

They ran into Prince Thomas at the library. It was a vast room with what looked like a thousand different books on hundreds of different subjects. Liz stared around in wonder at the curved glass walls, the bookshelves lining the inner walls, stretching from one large room and under an arch to another room of equal size and grandeur. Intricate carved designs covered the ceiling and anywhere lacking shelves. While she'd been staring open-mouthed around her, Arabella had sidled up to Thomas. The Princess suddenly popped her fist toward his gut, but he caught her arm and twisted it. Immediately, she swung at him with her other fist, which he grabbed with his other hand, bringing it behind her head. He held her like that for a moment with a triumphant grin, then released her, both of them laughing. Liz tilted her head; Thomas and Arabella were nothing like she'd imagined royalty would be. Instead, they were relaxed, friendly, and funny.

She almost leaned toward Liam to whisper her observation, but before the words left her lips, she realized that Liam had wandered over to the glass walls and was staring out over the Palace grounds, which they hadn't been able to see in daylight. Before Liz could join him, Arabella approached and, following his gaze, offered, "We could show you the gardens."

Liz, tired of seeing white-walled, painting-filled hallways with the occasional table, complete with a pink flower and blue vase, eagerly nodded. Liam silently joined them, his expression giving nothing away.

Eventually, after many hallways and even more stairs, they reached another glass door. Sunlight poured through it, making Liz blink rapidly until her eyes had adjusted. Outside, there were several bushes and hedges shaped like animals. Swans, giraffes, lions, elephants, bears... The list went on. A fountain with a stone dolphin gurgled nearby. On the edge of the fountain, reading a book, a young boy was sitting. He looked familiar, but it was several seconds before Liz could remember where she'd seen him before. It was Prince Henry, the youngest of Queen Isabella's three children.

"Great, " Graham murmured to Arabella. "The worm's here."

Arabella sighed. "I was hoping he'd still be inside stuffing his face with pastries." In a louder voice, she called, "Henry, what are you doing out here?"

The young Prince looked up, clearly annoyed. Holding up his book, he said in a snobby voice, "What does it look like I'm doing? I'm reading. You don't own the gardens, you know. I'm allowed to be out here too. I'm allowed to be anywhere I want." His little blue eyes found Liz and Liam, both standing uncomfortably behind Arabella and Graham. "Oh, you're showing *them* around? You're not usually so considerate to the fresh meat."

"Henry," Arabella said warningly. "Leave them alone."

"Why should I?" He let out a dramatic gasp. "Unless... you haven't told them. Oh, that would explain everything. Especially why they're following you around like you actually care about them."

"What's he talking about?" Liz whispered to Liam. Liam shrugged, eyes suspiciously narrowed.

"Shut up, Henry," Arabella ordered. Turning back toward the Palace and beckoning to Liz and Liam, she mumbled, "Let's beat it, guys."

Liz took a step after her then realized that Liam wasn't following them.

"What are you guys hiding from us?" Liam demanded, staring at Henry.

"*I'm* hiding nothing," Henry said smugly. "It's her you need to keep an eye on. Don't turn your back on *Arabella*, because she'll turn you over without a second thought."

Arabella stopped walking but didn't so much as look back at them as she snarled, "Henry. This has nothing to do with you. *Stop.*"

Liam looked at Arabella for a moment, then he carefully regarded Henry again. "Tell me. What do you mean?"

With a scornful look at Arabella, Henry stood up. "I told you I wasn't hiding anything, and she obviously hasn't told you. It's only fair that you know." He paused for dramatic effect. Liz just stared wide-eyed at him, her heart pounding as hundreds of scenarios went through her head. But for all of those situations she imagined, none could have hit her as hard as what he said.

"You're not here for training. You're *prisoners*. You're here so Alyspar can hand you over to the demons."

Chapter 9

WITHIN A SECOND, ARABELLA HAD WHIRLED AROUND furiously, charged at Henry, and decked him in the face. He fell backwards into the fountain water, his eyes watering. Liz covered her mouth, open in a silent gasp, while Liam stared on with wide eyes. Graham was looking at Arabella with a mixture of admiration and surprise. The only sound was the splash of Henry hitting the water. A few bubbles came up as he struggled to sit up, his hand pressed hard against his cheek. Once he came back up from the water, he gripped the edge of the fountain where he'd been sitting, leaning over it with his eyes screwed up in pain. With the sound of water dripping from his soaked clothes was his low moan of pain.

Arabella was still, visibly trembling. No one moved.

Liam was the first to recover. "What do you mean?" he

demanded, looking at Henry. Henry didn't answer, instead letting out a small sob. Liam turned to Arabella, who was still facing away from them. "What did he mean?" he insisted, raising his voice.

Arabella whipped around and swept away toward the Palace without answering or even looking at them. Graham quickly followed her, astonishment in his eyes. Liz gazed sightlessly at the fountain where Henry was crying. Given Arabella's reaction, there must have been some truth to what Henry had said. Starting to shake with nervousness, Liz dragged her eyes to Liam, who was glaring at Arabella's back.

Arabella and Graham stopped, Graham asking Arabella something in a soft voice. He flinched as she yelled back, "I don't make the rules! Okay?"

"But you must be able to do something –"

"What am I supposed to do? I'm so *sick* of watching my mother bring people to the Palace just to give their lives away, like they're worth nothing!"

Liz could feel her body growing weak, her vision swimming. She was hardly aware of Liam taking steps toward Henry, demanding, "What, does that mean – they're going to kill my sister?" Henry raised his head enough to look at Liam. With a glance at Arabella, he warily nodded. The Princess, however, was too focused on her argument with Graham to hear him.

Henry met Liam's eyes. "They do it to all of the Chosen. Give them a few days to get comfortable, and then they take them away." Liz looked at Arabella, hardly registering the angry tears streaming down her face. Graham was desperately trying to calm her down to no avail. Overwhelmed, Liz threw an abhorred look at Henry.

"You're a liar!" she spat in denial. "They wouldn't have brought me all this way just to – just to give my life away!"

"What do you know?" Henry said viciously, finally dropping his hand from his face and pulling himself out of the fountain.

"What do *you* know? You're, like, twelve!" Liz retorted.

"Fourteen, actually," he corrected her.

"As if it makes a difference!"

"I still know a right lot more than you do!"

Arabella suddenly burst out, "Shut up!" Everyone was instantly silent, though the tension between Liz and Henry remained as they glared at each other. Arabella walked to stand next to Liz, her eyes red and puffy. Graham hesitantly followed her. "You," Arabella growled at Henry, "get out of here before I really hurt you." He was quick to oblige, running to the door of the Palace and disappearing from sight. Arabella looked daggers at Liz. Liz took a shaky step back, startled by the intensity of Arabella's gaze. "And you... I'm not letting this happen again. Other countries don't sacrifice their Chosen. We shouldn't have to either."

"You mean you're going to help us?" Liam said carefully, sounding dubious. Liz, still in shock, felt her knees getting weaker. Falling to the ground with a moan, she tuned out of the conversation, staring into space. They had no choice but to accept Arabella's help. But the feeling of betrayal stung Liz still. The Princess had known everything. But even so... she was their only hope of escaping.

When Liz found herself able to focus again, she saw the other three looking down at her with concern. "Are you okay?" Liam asked. Liz blearily nodded. Liam added, "Did you hear her?" with a jerk of his head toward Arabella.

Looking at the Princess, Liz mumbled, "No... S-sorry?"

"I'll tell you later at the feast tonight," Arabella said quietly, blankly looking at the ground. Without emotion, "It will be too loud for anyone else to hear us. You never know who's out here."

Graham watched Arabella apprehensively as Liam helped Liz to her feet again. She still felt faint, but it looked like nothing compared to the emptiness Arabella seemed to be feeling. Finally, after moments of tense silence, Arabella lifted her head fiercely again, her eyes hard and determined. "Alright," she said decisively, turning to lead them back to the Palace. "Let's go."

"Tonight," Queen Isabella's voice boomed, "we celebrate the coming of our next Chosen!" She gripped Liz's hand and raised it high into the air. The height difference was apparent in that Liz had to stand on her toes to keep her shoulder from being pulled out of its socket. A great chorus of deafening cheers rose from the people at the feast. Liz winced, resisting the urge to cover her ears.

She'd been trying hard not to think about Henry's words, but she'd felt sick all day. Being with the Queen didn't help whatsoever. This was the woman who planned to sacrifice her to demons. The woman who'd lied, saying that Liz was here to train. Liz still didn't fully understand why she had to be sacrificed to appease the demons.

The Queen let go of Liz's hand, which she immediately dropped back to her side. With a surreptitious glance at Arabella, sitting next to Liz, she sat back down at the Royal Table. Liam was sitting at one of the longer tables with whom Queen Isabella referred to as the "privileged commoners". Graham sat next to him. Liz gave a worried look at Liam, but her brother had a steely look in his eyes as he looked back at her. Subdued even further, she looked down at the plate in front of her.

Trying to eat made her feel even worse. Her stomach was doing flips, and her head was pounding with apprehension. Eventually, she gave up, leaving her plate almost full. The Queen gave her a disapproving glance and sat up straighter.

Finally, the Queen and the King beside her, who was scarcely talked about because Queen Isabella did all of the ruling, moved to the empty room on the side and began to dance. Alone with Arabella, Liz felt a bit more relaxed, though she still couldn't manage to even swallow. Unsure of how much trust she could place in Arabella, after finding out that the Princess had known all along about the plan to sacrifice Liz, Liz knew that she was the only hope of escape. Arabella beckoned to Graham, who nudged Liam, and they all gathered behind the Royal Table, sitting close together.

"Okay," Arabella whispered, exchanging a glance with

Graham. Before she could say anything else, Liz felt a sudden surge of emotion and began trembling.

"Who all knows about this – how the Chosen are sacrificed, anyway?" she burst out.

With a frightful glance around them, Arabella answered quietly, "Lower your voice! We can't have anyone overhearing us. Hardly anyone knows. Just the royal family and some weird council my mother's in, I think."

"Why are Chosen sacrificed in the first place?" Liz demanded, not giving her time to say anything else.

"No one really knows why it works," Arabella said impatiently. "All we know is that if we take the Chosen to a greater demon's Gate and sacrifice them there, the greater demon can't come here from the Other World anymore." A thoughtful look flashed across her face. "I bet that council knows more than they let on. If we could just find something there, we could figure out everything they know…" Trailing off, she shook her head as if to clear it. "Sorry, but that's not the point. We have to get you out of here and to somewhere you'll be safe."

"Is there anywhere in Alyspar that the Queen doesn't hold so much power?" Liam asked in a low voice. "Anywhere Liz and I can go without her knowing?" Graham and Arabella exchanged a weighted glance, and Liz realized that they'd been talking seriously about this since their confrontation with Henry.

"Not in Alyspar…" Graham murmured slowly.

"What does that mean?" Liam snapped.

"We have to take you to Cujan," Arabella breathed.

"Cujan?" Liz yelped in surprise. It was no secret that there had been high tension between Alyspar and Cujan for the last decade. No one really questioned why but assumed it had to do with the difference in government. Cujan was a democracy with no clear leader, just an elected council that changed out every four years.

"Yes, Cujan," Arabella confirmed patiently. "I know it's a stretch, and it's dangerous, but–"

"Dangerous?" Liz repeated.

Liam raised his eyebrows. "It's more than dangerous. How are we supposed to get across the border? What if Cujan kills us on sight? What if the Queen finds out?" Suddenly narrowing his eyes, which had turned dark, he asked, "What if *you* tell her?"

Arabella gave him an even stare. In a flat voice, she answered, "I'm not telling my mother anything. Graham and I are coming with you." Liz stared at her in wonder. Did she want to get away from her mother that much? So much that she would abandon her own country? Arabella added, "They'll let us across the border because I'm the Princess. Especially if I tell them what my mother's been doing. Cujan was one of the first countries to look for an alternative to the sacrifices."

"So what are you kiddos talking about?" A voice behind them made them all jump. They looked around in a panic, but it was just Thomas. "You're being awfully secretive, what with the whispering and all." His eyes were suspiciously

111

narrowed. Arabella shrugged at him, her gaze sharp. They stared each other down for a few seconds before a look of understanding came over Thomas's face. "You're leaving."

Arabella shrugged again and looked away. "It's none of your business."

"Hey now," Thomas's voice held a note of warning. "It is my business if my sister is giving up on Alyspar. I know you've disagreed with Mom about a lot, but so have I. That doesn't mean I'm abandoning my country."

Arabella gave him a fierce look. "I'm not letting her take anyone else's life away from them because she's too stubborn to figure something else out like everyone else has."

"She's not the only one who's stubborn," Thomas grumbled, then let out a sigh. "But I won't stop you. It's your decision. I've liked you two from the beginning anyway," he added with a serious look at Liz and Liam. "Just be careful getting out of here. When are you planning?" Arabella and Graham looked at each other again, and Graham nodded reassuringly.

"Tomorow. Before Mom has the chance to take Liz away," Arabella told him.

Thomas sighed again. "Okay. Just... be safe, alright? Don't get yourself killed trying to get away. You know that it won't be as simple as walking out." Arabella had tears in her eyes. Jumping up, she gave Thomas a tight hug, which he returned.

"Thank you," she murmured so quietly that Liz almost didn't hear what she said. "You're the best big brother I could've wished for."

"And you're the best little sister I could've wished for," Thomas said warmly. "I admire you, you know. For getting yourself out of this mess."

They shared a few more quiet words before Thomas nodded to them all and walked away.

Once he'd wandered off, Arabella rejoined them. She opened her mouth to say something but snapped it shut again, looking over Liz's shoulder. Turning around, Liz saw Queen Isabella walking back toward them.

"We'll get you out of here tomorrow," Graham promised quickly, and then the Queen was sitting next to them once more.

"Bella," the Queen summoned her daughter and gave a hostile look at Graham, Liam, and Liz. The three of them, frustrated by the interruption, moved away from the Royal Table and allowed the Queen and Princess to speak privately.

As they sat at the far end of one of the long tables, Graham murmured, "We can't get away without her…"

"Why not?" Liam demanded. "Why should we trust her or you?" Liz shivered as he echoed her own thoughts.

Graham turned to face him. "How do you expect to get across the border without her? How do you expect to even leave the Palace without her? Tell me where there weren't guards, because that would make this whole situation a lot easier." Looking back at Arabella, he added softly, "There are guards all over the place, at every entrance. If you're smart, you'll wait for her. She's your only hope."

Arabella was starting to look agitated, her arms crossed

with an expression of stone. Queen Isabella had risen to her feet, but Liz couldn't hear what she was saying. Then the Queen beckoned to Seth and another Royal Guard. She said something to them, and they both looked over at Graham, Liz, and Liam. With a nod, Seth and the other Royal Guard began to walk over to them. Arabella jumped after them, shouting something that Liz couldn't hear, but her mother snagged her arm and didn't let go.

For a moment, Liz was happy to see Seth again, but his grave expression cut her greeting short. When he reached them, he hoisted Liz up by her shoulders. Letting out a gasp of surprise, Liz struggled against his grip, but he pulled her out into the hallway, Liam and Graham on his heels. Her last glimpse of the feast was of Arabella being forcefully tugged back by her mother after trying to run after them.

Liam stepped in front of Seth with alarming ferocity. "Let her go."

"Queen's orders," Seth said with a note of apology in his voice. "You and your sister are to be confined to your quarters until tomorrow. Then Liz will begin her training as one of the Chosen."

Liam looked like he was about to say something else when the other Royal Guard constricted his arms behind his back and pulled him down the other hallway. "Wait!" he shouted, but his voice was drowned out by the sounds of the feast. Gradually his shouts faded. Graham hastily followed Seth.

"Don't do this," he pleaded. "Don't you see? She's not starting her Chosen training tomorrow, she's going to be taken away and sacrificed!"

Seth's steps faltered, but only for a moment. "Where in the world did you hear that? That's ridiculous."

"The Queen doesn't train Chosen, she kills them," Graham said urgently. "She–"

"Don't speak so lowly of the Queen!" Seth snapped. "I've pledged my life to serve her, and so have you as a Royal Guard in training. Or did you forget about that? Anyway, she would never treat her own subjects with such injustice."

Graham had to trot at Seth's side to keep up. Liz was stumbling along on his other side, too afraid to try escaping his firm hold on her. Graham insisted, "I wouldn't have believed it either, but today Henry told us everything, and Arabella said he wasn't lying. I believe the Princess."

"Yes, we all know how you feel about her," Seth said impatiently, not sparing so much as a glance toward Graham. Seeming annoyed, he didn't say anything and kept walking. Graham hesitated.

He brought his fist up as if to punch Seth. In an instant, Seth had pushed Liz to the floor, out of harm's way, and adopted a fighting stance. Graham and Seth stared at each other for a few tense moments. Then, behind Graham, another Royal Guard was rushing toward them. Seth dropped his fists as Graham was restrained. Liz climbed to her feet, but before she could get away from Seth, he grabbed her arm again.

"Don't do this," Graham begged.

Seth shook his head and sighed. "I'm sorry, to both of you." As he led Liz away, she could hear Graham pulling againt the Royal Guard's grip, but to no avail. They came to Liz's room, which she still couldn't recognize based on the hallway and door alone. Seth opened the door. "I'm sorry," he repeated. "But the Queen wants you to stay here. It's for your own safety. To reassure you, she wanted me to tell you that there are guards positioned all throughout the grounds and everywhere inside the Palace. You'll be allowed out in the morning for breakfast." And with that, he was gone.

"My own safety?" Liz scoffed quietly, feeling tears welling up in her eyes. "Sure. Sure, it's for my own safety." She dropped onto the bed and closed her eyes, drowning in misery.

The doors were in Liz's dreams that night. The boy that had recently been appearing next to the doors was nowhere to be found, though she looked. His presence had felt familiar to her, and right now familiarity was something she dearly missed. She missed Koln. She missed her mother.

And now she missed Liam too.

The doors shook and trembled. Liz blankly stared at them. Maybe it would be better if she just let them open. Maybe she shouldn't run away. Maybe they could take this pain away.

A loud knock woke her up before the doors could open. Running her fingers through her hair, she got up and reluctantly answered the door. A Royal Guard was standing there.

"You have ten minutes to get ready, and then it's off to breakfast." His tone was cold, but there was sympathy in his eyes.

Liz splashed some cold water on her face, trying to rub the feeling of tears off. Looking in the mirror, she saw that the demon's scratches on her face had scabbed over. She'd almsot forgotten about them. Thankfully, they no longer hurt.

She listlessly followed the Royal Guard down to the Dining Hall and numbly entered the room. It was a bit early for breakfast, and the room was nearly deserted. Liam and Graham were nowhere to be seen. Food covered the tables at the back of the room. Liz saw donuts, pastries, cereals, and fruit, though her appetite was minuscule. A variety of juices were also available. The Royal Guard gestured to the food and drinks then went to stand by the door. He attentively watched Liz with suspicious eyes as if waiting for her to try to escape. Liz started to walk to a table with her chosen food when her eyes traveled across the room and saw someone she'd thought was dead.

The Prophet.

Chapter 10

THE PROPHET'S EYES LAZILY DRIFTED OVER TO LIZ.
Old and wrinkled, her dark skin aged with countless years,
the Prophet looked like she hadn't changed since Liz had first
seen her all those years ago. The ancient woman reached out
a crooked finger and beckoned to her – a sight that reminded
her of seeing the Prophet in the shadows of the Old People's
Home. It seemed like such a long time ago now, though it had
only been a few weeks. So many things had changed, all at a
moment's notice.

Tentatively, Liz walked over to the Prophet's table and
stopped on the opposite side, unsure of what to do. Should
she sit down? Should she have answered the Prophet's summons in the first place?

"So you made it here," the Prophet croaked. "Good,
good…"

"I thought you were dead… What do you want from me?" Liz asked warily.

"I don't want anything from you," the Prophet said in a slow drawl. "I just want you to be safe."

"Since you first talked to me, everything has – nothing good has happened," Liz told her. Hesitating, she added, "Where's my mom?"

The Prophet's eyes remained vacant. "You mean Alina? She didn't make it."

Liz felt her heart drop down into her stomach. In the back of her mind, she'd kind of known that Alina had died. No one could have escaped from the demons' destruction. Still, she had been holding onto the hope that her mother had made it. Liz lowered her eyes.

"Ah!" the Prophet wheezed with a small twinkle in her eyes. "But you did. And now you have a very important job to do. Where's Liam?"

Liz didn't answer her. Her chest had caved in, and she was having difficulties simply breathing. Alina was gone forever. Liz could hardly stand the thought of never seeing her again. There had been many arguments between them, but now Liz regretted each and every one more than ever before.

"Liz. Where's Liam?" the Prophet repeated, the twinkle in her eyes vanishing like morning dew in sunshine. "We don't have much time. You need to tell me."

Trying to talk around the lump in her throat, Liz murmured, "I…I don't know anymore." Her voice sounded soft and distant, as though it were coming from someone else.

Suddenly, she felt a spark of anger rise within her, and she tried to keep her voice level as she asked, "Why did you lie to us?"

"Lie to you about what, child?" the Prophet asked, once again sounding cold and disinterested.

"About Liam being...*chosen*," she spat the word.

The Prophet narrowed her eyes. "You only assumed I meant Liam," she said slowly.

"No..." Liz protested, racking her brain. "You said...You said that my brother was Chosen!"

"He is." A pause. "And Liam is too, perhaps even more Chosen than you are..."

"But Liam *is* my brother," Liz insisted coldly, trying to ignore a small flicker of doubt. She'd thought that the prophet had been lying when she'd said that Liz was Chosen, but that had turned out to be true. Maybe what the Prophet was implying was true too. Liz added, partly in an attempt to convince herself, "If he's not my brother, who is? Wouldn't I have noticed something if he wasn't?"

The Prophet blinked in slow motion. "Think about your dreams. You're so pale you could blend in with the snow. He and Alina both are tan, their skin brown without needing the sun."

"My mom always told me that I look like my dad, that's all," Liz countered flatly.

"She was lying." The Prophet sighed. "Alyspar never was good at handling their Chosen. Always keeping them in the dark..."

"Stop talking in riddles!" Liz cried in exasperation. "If you have something to say to me, just say it, please! Is Liam my brother or isn't he?"

"No," the Prophet murmured, closing her eyes. "You two are not related at all. It was the false family you were placed in to keep you safe."

"Safe from what?" was the first thing that came out of Liz's mouth. Then realization kicked in, and it felt like the ground itself had just caved in from underneath her feet. Like she was floating in endless space. Her entire life had been a lie? Memories flashed through her mind, every moment with Liam and Alina that she could remember. How could they lie to her? Her stomach felt like it was folding in on itself, a familiar feeling to her by now. So many tears had fallen from her face in the last week that she could no longer cry, though the urge was strong now. "So…" she said slowly, not hearing if the Prophet had even answered her first question. "Alina… She's not my mom?"

The Prophet shook her head, opening her old eyes again.

"But how could they just – how could they lie to me like that?" Liz burst, angry tears finally flowing down her face. "Like it's nothing? Like…Like I'm nothing…?"

"It's part of the agreement," the Prophet wheezed before having a small coughing fit. Before Liz could question her again, she continued, "Whenever a family takes in one of the Chosen, they sign an agreement not to reveal any more than what's necessary. Some Chosen go their entire lives without knowing the truth. Unfortunately, you became necessary to the country."

"What, it became 'necessary' to murder me?" Liz snapped. People around the Dining Hall were beginning to give them weird looks, but Liz found that she didn't care anymore. "Nothing justifies murder, nothing!"

Light footsteps behind her made her whirl around, full of rage and ready to punch whatever was coming toward her. A sick feeling of satisfaction came over her when she saw that it was Liam, who caught on to her anger and stopped several feet away. He peered past her to see the Prophet, hostility coming into his eyes. "What are *you* doing here? Liz, what's she said to you?"

"Don't call me that!" Liz snarled. By now, everyone in the Dining Hall had stopped to watch the unfolding scene. "You lied to me!" Liz stepped forward, ready to punch Liam. There was no dawning realization in his eyes, no guilt or shame. How dare he? "I bet you thought it was really funny, didn't you, acting like we were one big, happy family? 'Oh, it's just *Elizabeth*, she doesn't need to know anything!' Is that even my real name?" She advanced on him, raising her fists.

"He didn't know, Elizabeth," the Prophet croaked from behind her. Liz's fists faltered, and she glared distrustfully at Liam. The Prophet added, "He was only two when you were placed there for safekeeping."

"Then you," Liz rounded on the Prophet. "You knew, all that time, and you never said anything!"

"I was part of the agreement too," the Prophet told her. "I was forbidden to tell you. I also signed an agreement to keep you – the both of you – safe. It was with Liam's father. The Queen had no part in that. I think you should know that."

"So…" Liam spoke again. "That's why I was brought here too, because of your agreement. That's why the Queen didn't know who I am."

The Prophet nodded. Liz and Liam stared at her for a moment. Liz was trying to process everything the Prophet had said. She looked back at Liam. He really had believed that he was her brother. And just like that, the anger faded as she thought of how good he'd been at being a big brother. But his appearance contrasted so greatly with Liz's ghostly-pale skin and small frame. It had never bothered her before, but now he just reminded her of Alina and the secrets she'd kept. Prickles of anger returned deep inside of her. The rapid mix of emotions made her feel like she was going to throw up.

"Liz, what's she talking about?" Liam asked, taking a tentative step forward. "Is this about Mom? What's going on?"

Liz just stared at him, her eyes still brimming with tears. "She's… Your mom is gone," she struggled to say. Despite her anger toward Alina, she couldn't forget how her false mother had raised her. Well, raised her to the age of fifteen. Now… she had no one.

Liam's eyes widened, "No." He looked at the Prophet, not blinking.

The Prophet returned his gaze steadily, her expression impossible to read, but it seemed to tell Liam everything he needed to know. Tears formed in his eyes and fell down his cheek, though he rapidly blinked in an attempt to keep them at bay.

"Why…" he choked out, wiping the tears from his face. "Why did you say…*my* mom?"

Liz felt so disconnected from her own body that she didn't recognize the voice as her own and was half-convinced that the Prophet was now speaking through her. "She's not my mom. You're not my brother."

He glared past her at the Prophet, still fending off tears. "Will you stop lying to my sister?"

"She's not your sister, Liam," the Prophet said gently.

"No, you're a liar! You lied when you said I was Chosen, and you're lying now!"

"I've told you nothing but the truth. It's time you both knew."

"No!" Liam protested again. "You said we were both Chosen, and we were both special, but guess what? That wasn't the truth!"

"Jealousy is a part of human nature," the Prophet said, remaining aloof, "albeit an ugly part. One day soon you'll understand. You both have significance in your futures."

"What is there to understand?" Liam stepped toward the Prophet, towering above her. She still sat there, not looking at him, holding a coffee cup up to her lips. He insisted, "You lied to us then, and you're lying to us now!"

"Child," the Prophet chastised, "you know nothing of what you're talking about. You think you're not Chosen? You're even more Chosen than Elizabeth, even if not from Xanedur. You don't know what makes a person Chosen, and I have a feeling that I won't get to tell you today." She glanced around the room, and Liz followed her gaze. People all over the room were staring, looking confused and startled. Over at the door, the guards were speaking with each other in hushed voices, concerned. One of them nodded and left the room. The other one raised his voice.

"Everyone out. This is classified. Not you two," he said sternly, pointing at Liz and Liam when they began to move for the door. The Prophet watched them as they sat down, casting her hostile looks.

The Dining Hall seemed too large for just four people. It was eerily silent with the guard staring them down and the Prophet sipping her coffee without a sound. Several minutes passed before anything happened, during which Liz could feel cold sweat on her face and her whole body shaking nervously. Then the other Royal Guard came back with – who else? – Queen Isabella following him. Behind her, another Royal Guard came into the room.

Queen Isabella strolled over to them, her eyes critical as she considered them. Her hair was wrapped up in a large bun at the upper back of her head, her elegant red dress reaching all the way to the floor. Her icy blue eyes lingered on Liz for an extra moment, causing Liz to inwardly shiver. Finally, Queen Isabella crossed her arms and let out a heavy sigh. Pointing a careless finger at the Prophet, she ordered, "Remove this woman."

"Where should we put her, Your Highness?" the guard asked as he roughly pulled the old woman from her chair.

She dropped her coffee mug, which shattered on the floor.

The Queen shrugged. "Just get her out of my sight. I've wanted her off the council for years, now I finally have an excuse."

The Prophet rested her eyes on the Queen, and for the first time, Liz thought she saw a glimmer of emotion in them. "I guess our history means nothing to you then."

A furious look came over Queen Isabella's face. Without responding, she snapped, "Put her in the prison block."

The guard wordlessly nodded and dragged the Prophet out of the room. She didn't even look at Liz as she was forced away. Liz's heart sank, realizing that she would probably never see the Prophet again. She hadn't gotten to ask all of the questions she had. Who else could explain what the Prophet had meant?

The Prophet vanished from sight, and in her place, Arabella strode into view. Catching sight of them in the Dining Hall, she sharply turned and marched into the room, stopping just short of the Queen. Graham was right behind her, running to catch up. Throwing her arms out at her sides, Arabella breathlessly cried, "Mom, I've been looking everywhere for you! Someone broke into your room! The lock's broken off, one of the doors is off its hinges –"

"What?" Queen Isabella hissed, rounding on Arabella. "How convenient!" Without another word, she swept out of the room. The guards made to follow her but quickly resumed their posts when she venomously spat, "Don't leave them! I'll take care of this." And the Queen was gone.

Arabella stared after her for a few moments before giving Liz and Liam a significant look, as if she were trying to tell them something. Then she started to leave the room, Graham waiting for her at the door. Liz blinked, and in that moment, Arabella had smashed her elbow into one of the guards' face. In the same instant, Graham had slammed his fist into the other guard's temple, knocking him out.

"Well, come on then!" Arabella urged as the guards twitched on the floor. Liz dumbly watched the Princess, her mouth agape. After learning that Alina was dead and that Liam wasn't her brother, she was already in shock. Moving seemed impossible.

"Guys, we have to move!" Graham shook Liz by her shoulders, and she felt herself stand up. Her legs moved without her consciously telling them to, Liam on her heels. Arabella glanced both ways down the hallway and, seeing no one, sprinted to the left. Liz had a hard time keeping up with her. She heard Liam huffing behind her and knew that he was having difficulties too. Graham took up the rear, checking behind them every few seconds.

They turned down one hallway after another. Liz had no idea where they were or how anyone knew where they were going in the Palace. It was like a huge maze. She, breathing heavily, gasped, "Where are we going?"

Without pausing for breath, Arabella said, "We're getting you out of here." They sped around a servant, who made an alarmed noise and jumped out of the way. The servant stared after them, aghast, before they turned another corner, leaving the servant behind.

By the time they skidded around a corner and saw a door leading outside, Liz's sides felt like they were on fire, and her legs felt weak. But without the slightest pause, Arabella threw open the doors and, still at an unhalting run, led them toward a large, gray building just north of the Palace. It looked like a warehouse with huge tin doors that opened upward. Arabella pressed a sizeable button, and the doors trembled. Liz was momentarily thrown into the memory of her dreams, filled with the black doors – Xanedur's Gate, opening to vast blackness. Then the tin doors in front of her began to open, and she was thrust back into the present, a single bead of sweat trickling down her face.

Arabella tried to look casual as they waited for the doors to open, glancing around at the people milling about nearby. None of them paid their group any attention. Graham impatiently tapped his hand on his leg, staring at the doors. After what seemed like forever, the doors were open enough for Arabella to slide underneath, leading the others into the warehouse. Liz didn't know where she was going or what they were doing. All she knew was that the Princess was her only hope at getting away from the Queen.

Inside the warehouse, cars lined the walls with numbers printed above them. In the corner was a spacious office with a wall filled with keys. Arabella grabbed a key, checked the number, and ran out of the office, frantically looking around the warehouse until she spotted the matching number. Beckoning to them, she sprinted to the car marked "34". They piled into the car, Liz and Liam in the back with Graham in the passenger seat. Arabella was driving.

"Have you ever driven before?" Liam asked with a nervous chuckle. Arabella jammed the key into the ignition and pressed her foot against the gas pedal. Without moving, the car's engine revved, echoing around the warehouse. Turning red, she clumsily moved the gear shift and hit the gas again. The car lurched backward toward the wall, and Arabella slammed her foot against the break with a nervous laugh.

"Once, that's got to count for something, right?" she said, her voice quick and quiet.

"*Once?*" Liz cried before they sped from the warehouse, tires screeching. As they passed the Palace doors, barely missing pedestrians, Seth and another Royal Guard burst outside. They wildly looked around before spotting the single car racing away from the warehouse. Just before they went around a corner, Liz saw the Royal Guards run toward the warehouse, hysterically shouting to each other.

Arabella seemed calmer as they rocketed through the Palace grounds, the car shifting one way and then the other as she tried to keep control of it. Seeing the alarm in Graham's eyes, she breathed, "Sue me. I've always been driven around in a limo." She still sounded nervous, but she had a fiery look in her eyes as they approached the Palace walls. Regaining her composure, she put on a smile that looked genuine when they came to a halt before the closed gate. A small gray building stood off to the side, from which a couple of guards came out.

"Princess Arabella," one of the guards said when they reached the car, the surprise evident in his voice. "You are driving." He shook his head, trying to clear the shock off of his face. "On what business do you wish to leave the Palace grounds? And are those two – isn't she Chosen? Where are you all going?"

"I just wanted to show them around downtown," Arabella said innocently. "Get some funnel cakes before they have to go train as Chosen, you know? I promise we won't get into any trouble…" Arabella's eyes sparkled with hope.

"Ah. You're not up to any mischief now, are you?" the guard teased, his stern look melting into a smile. "Well, alright. Can't argue against the Princess's orders. Lift the gates!" he shouted to the other guards. One of the guards by the side of the gray building nodded and pulled a large lever beside the gate. The gate began to open as another guard ran from the building, looking alarmed.

"No, wait, don't let them through!" he cried, just as the gate was high enough for their car to fit underneath. Arabella sped through before they could react, all of the guards watching them go with startled faces. There was no stopping them now. Liz let out a nervous laugh, realizing that she'd been holding her breath from the moment they'd left the Palace. This was it.

She was free.

Chapter 11

AFTER A FEW RELIEVED MOMENTS, LIZ REALIZED SHE WASN'T free quite yet.

"Alright…" Liam said slowly after several tense minutes of silence. They were driving through the northern upper district now, leaving the Palace far behind. "We appreciate how you got us out of the Palace and all… But now how are we going to get out of Aloria? Aren't there guards at the wall?"

"I know a guy," Arabella assured them. "And we're not going to the wall."

"Then where are we going?" Liam asked. Liz hardly heard him. Everything felt distant as she stared out at the houses flashing by.

Graham answered from somewhere far away, "We didn't quite work out the details with everyone we meant to, but…"

"So, uh, what are you going to tell them once they've caught us?" Liam asked a little too loudly, sirens suddenly whining in the distance behind them. The Queen had sent the police after them. Graham looked at Arabella expectantly. Meeting his solid gaze for an instant, Arabella said with certainty, "We won't get caught." After a few moments, she added, "Anyway, so what if it's not a perfect plan? We didn't have time, we had to do *something*. My mom was going to take Liz away today!"

"Wait… Was that a lie, about the Queen's room being broken into?" Liam asked. Liz hadn't even made that connection. All of her thoughts had flown out of her head when the Prophet had told her about everything in her life being a total lie from the very beginning.

"Not entirely…" Arabella answered slowly, focusing on the road as they turned a sharp corner entirely too fast. "Graham and I kicked the door down and threw some stuff around. We found some files in there too…" Readjusting her grip on the steering wheel, she glanced at them in the rearview mirror. "They, uh… They say some pretty fascinating stuff, wouldn't you say, Graham?" Her voice held a note of nervousness, higher than usual.

Graham looked at her with wide eyes. "Uh, yeah, they do. We'll… We'll show you when we're in a safer place."

Liz silently watched the huge mansions of the upper district flash by at a speed that was probably unsafe. Especially because Arabella wasn't an experienced driver. They kept jerking this way and that as she struggled to maintain control of the car.

Arabella glanced back at them again for a moment. "We'll

have to ditch the car and run on foot soon, lose their trail. The police are after us, and probably all of the Royal Guards too." The sirens continued to wail in the distance, but they were certainly getting closer. Liz continued to listlessly stare out the window.

The car lurched to a sudden stop, throwing Liz forward. She hadn't even thought about wearing the seatbelt, as this was her second time ever in a car, the first being the limousine on the way to the Palace a couple of days prior. She saw that Liam had also slammed into Arabella's seat. Liz watched as he pulled himself up and opened the car door, getting out. At the urgent call of Arabella, Liz slowly got out of the car to join them.

"Liz," Liam said sternly as he pulled her after Arabella and Graham, who had already started to run. "You have to snap out of it. We can't afford to have you fall behind." There was a strangely unfamiliar gleam in his eyes that Liz couldn't identify.

She stared at his hand, gripping her arm to steer her in the right direction. Feeling a sudden surge of anger, she pulled away. "Let go of me, I know how to run!" she snapped. Startled, he paused, shook his head, and sprinted after Arabella and Graham. Liz followed them.

Arabella and Graham kept glancing over their shoulders, urging them on. The running began to feel routine, but Liz's sides were still burning after only a few moments. She stumbled and came to a stop, panting painfully.

"You okay?" Arabella called from the front of their group,

slowing down.

"My sides," Liz gasped, holding a hand to her left side where the pain was worst.

"Hey," Arabella offered. "Time your breaths with your steps. Every two steps breathe in, then two again and breathe out."

"We have to hurry!" Graham's voice was impatient, reluctantly slowing down for them to catch up. "We have to get out of here."

While Arabella's advice didn't seem to help at first, Liz noticed that the pain in her sides wasn't getting worse. Though she'd been doubtful at first, she suddenly felt grateful that of all people who could be helping her escape, it was the Princess and her apparent best friend.

Graham and Arabella sounded rushed, but they didn't seem worried. Instead, Graham's eyes shone with excitement as he grinned back at Liz. Arabella's face wore an expression of pure hatred. Liz guessed that she was thinking about her mother. Meanwhile, the sirens were definitely getting closer. They must have found the car already.

Soon, Liz could smell salt in the air and realized that they must be heading toward the ocean. While she'd known that they'd been heading north at first, she'd gotten turned around after their frantic drive through the upper district. As the ocean crossed her mind, she glimpsed the blue mass through the buildings ahead of them. Passing the last house on the block, they ran by an old man watering his lawn. He angrily shook a cane after them, shouting, "Hooligans!"

His wife, coming to stand beside him while shaking her head, added, "You kids will be the death of this country!"

They skirted around another building and narrowly avoided getting hit by a car, which skidded to a stop just inches from Arabella. The driver stared after them as they continued to run, then opened his window and called out, "Hey! Are those – are those sirens after *you*? The Princess?" The driver opened his car door and hesitated, then climbed back in and quickly drove off.

Arabella led them underneath a sign that had a big "36" dominating most of it. Ahead of them stretched long, wooden piers into the ocean, each with its own designated number. Most of the piers were empty, and at first glance this seemed to be a dead end. Liz halted, seeing only a small boat docked at pier thirty-six. The rest of the area was deserted, and thoughts of a trap crossed Liz's mind. Arabella called something out as they neared the single boat.

A young man – Liz guessed him to be nearly twenty – hurriedly limped off of the boat and approached them. Panicked, Liz thought that they'd been compromised, but then Arabella gave the man a quick hug and greeted him. "Thank you for helping us again, John."

Enthusiastically shaking Graham's hand, John said, "You made it! Didn't think you'd have the police on your tail, but you made it. You always were quite the troublemaker." He looked at Arabella with a mischievous gleam in his eyes. Then he seemed to notice Liz and Liam and appraised them, hands on his hips. After a few moments, he let out a boisterous laugh and seized Liz's hand, then Liam's. "You kids don't seem too bad."

Arabella rolled her eyes with a smirk, seeming more at ease now that they'd come to a stop. "We really need to get going before they find us."

Turning to give her a serious look, John's smile vanished. "Of course. Now, Arabella, I don't know why you're running from the Queen or why it's so important that you get these two out. I'm putting a lot of trust in you, lending you my boat, so you'd best not make me regret it." A pained look came into his eyes. "You know, after I lost my leg... You were the one who taught me to live without it. You've been a good friend, and I don't want to see you get hanged for treason."

Arabella didn't meet his eyes at first. "My mom doesn't know where we're going, I promise you. I would tell you, but..." She raised her eyes to his and said softly, "You'd be in enough trouble as it is if they found out you helped us get out of here. I don't want you getting hurt." She gave him one last hug, and the moment was gone.

"Graham?" Arabella said expectantly, turning to look at him. He was staring between her and John with a strange expression, but at her voice, he nodded and moved to the boat's controls. A soft roar issued from the engines.

As they began to drift away, John called out, "Take care of yourself, and your friends too, Bella."

"Thank you, John," she called back. "You're a literal life-saver. Now hurry and get out of here before they figure out where we went." With one last, grim smile, John turned, limped up the pier, and disappeared. Arabella watched after him for a moment and then turned to face Graham. "Well, guys, let's get out of here."

Soon enough, the boat was making its way across the water away from the shore. "This boat can't handle going too far from shore," Graham informed them, "so we'll have to hope that the guards at the wall aren't watching the water."

"Why aren't we going faster?" Liz muttered nervously, gazing apprehensively back at the shore. Any moment the police could come to the pier and see them. The sirens were still floating toward them as they left the pier behind.

Arabella answered, "If we move too fast, it will attract the guards' attention. It's better if we lay low while we get out of here."

Some time passed as they slowly moved north, parallel to the shore. Liz, having finally caught her breath, asked, "You're absolutely sure they don't know that we have a boat?" She was still shaking, her heart racing, though the steady hum of the boat was starting to calm her down.

"They'll figure it out eventually," Arabella sighed. "But we have a bit before they check the docks. John will have to report them that that his boat is missing so they don't think he was in on the plan. He's going to give us a day's head start," she added just as Liz opened her mouth to ask. Shutting it again, she stared across the water back at the capital, now far enough that she couldn't tell which pier was thirty-six.

"So... have you done this before?" Liam asked, calmly sitting at the back of the boat.

"Done what?" Arabella asked without looking at him. She and Graham were both keeping an eye on the walls of the city as they got closer.

"Run away. You seem very... enthusiastic."

Arabella let out a small laugh. "Guess it's the adrenaline. I've felt on my toes since I nailed that guard in the face."

They were quiet for a while, all holding their breath as they slowly passed by the wall. They were going slowly enough that they couldn't be heard from shore. None of them dared to even speak, but no alarm went off. The wall passed by them, and eventually they could no longer see the grand, corrupt walls of Aloria.

After they'd been past the walls for some time, Liam wondered out loud, just above the sound of the boat, "What about when we run out of gas?" His eyes were vacant as he looked out across the open ocean.

"We had John fill us up and pack some more in here for when we get low," Graham answered, sitting idly by the boat's controls.

"Graham's idea. I hadn't even thought of it," Arabella admitted, giving Graham an appreciative look. They lapsed into silence again, leaving each of them to their own thoughts.

The sun was shining directly down on them, heat beating down on their shoulders. Liam looked like he'd fallen asleep, his head lolling to the side. Liz was watching the shore of Alyspar as they sped past it. The land, at its distance, made it look like they were going slower than a snail's pace.

Arabella spoke in a low voice, perhaps only meaning for Graham to hear. "I can't believe I finally got away from my mother."

"Yeah..." Graham gave her a soft look. "I can't believe you trusted me to come with you."

"Who else would control the boat? I don't know how," Arabella laughed. Then she returned his gaze. "I wouldn't trust anyone else."

"Do you think you'll ever go back?"

"We'll be hanged for treason if we ever go back."

"I mean after Queen Isabella is gone. When Thomas is in charge."

"I'm hoping the monarchy will end," Arabella confessed. "It's outdated. Cujan's moved on and so has everywhere else. It's just not a good form of government anymore, if it ever was." She leaned against the railing of the boat. "Alyspar is corrupt, there's no denying it. All those people stuck in the lower district – even in the capital, and no one does anything to help them. It's not fair." Her voice had turned bitter. Graham looked at her sympathetically, and they resumed their silence.

It was beginning to get dark. Liam was still asleep, murmuring quietly off and on. Liz felt her eyelids flickering, and she knew that she would fall asleep soon as well. Graham never looked away from the open water in front of them except to occasionally glance back at Arabella. Liz yawned. She'd been tired since they'd passed the wall of Aloria – but she'd also been worried that the Queen had known where they were going and sent boats after them. Arabella approached her, and she looked up at the rebel Princess.

"I, uh... I found something in the Queen's room that you might be interested in," Arabella told her quietly. An uncertain look was in her eyes as she produced a folded up bunch of papers from her pocket, sorting through the sheets until she pulled one out and smoothed it. "I understand what makes people Chosen now. I don't think you'll like it."

"It can't be that bad, can it?" Liz asked nervously. She was tired of bad news and would've appreciated a break for a while. But whatever Arabella had to say had to be important, otherwise she wouldn't be bringing it up now.

"It's pretty bad," Arabella said, pity in her eyes. Liz's heart slowly fell yet again. Arabella took a deep breath and asked, "Are you ready?" Liz nodded, biting her lip. "Okay... The Chosen... People are Chosen because one of their parents is a demon."

Chapter 12

"WHAT?" LIZ HAD SURELY HEARD HER WRONG.

"It's your birth mom. She's a demon," Arabella said gently. Feeling dizzy, Liz sat down and covered her face with her hands. Arabella had to be wrong. There was no way she was part demon. *No one* was part demon. But then…it was the only explanation for anything she had.

"So… That's why I'm… different? My mom is a…" Liz couldn't bring herself to say it yet.

"There's more." Arabella offered Liz the folded up piece of paper, and Liz took it with a trembling hand. She dreaded looking at it, but she knew she had to. She had to know the truth.

In the top right corner, there were four pictures. The first one was of a small baby with dark hair and pale skin. Its eyes were closed. Underneath it was a label that said "6 months". The second picture, labeled "5 years", was of the same child, smiling over her shoulder as she played outside. Liz recognized the surroundings immediately – it was Koln. It was home. Feeling apprehensive, she dragged her eyes down to the next picture. Labeled "10 years", this was one of Liz's school pictures. The last picture was Liz's latest school picture. "15 years". Feeling sick, she moved her eyes to the writing beside the pictures. Arabella stood by, uncomfortably twiddling her thumbs.

Half-Demon Protection Agency
Person in Question: Rachel Marie Kline
Cover: Elizabeth Jewel Prower
Status: Alyspar citizen

Liz stared hard at her own name, trying to piece everything together. This was her file then. She remembered asking Liam if Elizabeth was even her real name. This single piece of paper answered that question. She blinked a couple of times. Too confused and tired to cry, she bit her lip.

All her life, things had been simple, and she'd been a normal person. Now, all of a sudden, her mother was a demon. It made her feel like a monster. She looked below that writing to the next few lines.

Father / status: Zachary Kline / Cujan citizen
Mother / status: Xanedur / demon

Sibling(s) / cover / status: Levi Hart Kline / Michael Lee Marshall / Cujan citizen

Liz stopped reading and searched the paper for something official to mark it as legitimate, feeling hopelessly suspicious. This *had* to be some sort of joke. In the bottom right corner, there was a small seal marked with HDPA. With a glance at the top of the paper, Liz figured that that stood for Half-Demon Protection Agency. If it was fake, there was no way she could tell. She turned her eyes down to the words below what she'd already read.

"Rachel Marie Kline, under the cover name Elizabeth Jewel Prower, has been relocated from Avery, Cujan, to Koln, Alyspar. She will be placed with the Prower family (Milon Usher Prower / Alina Catherine Prower), as they have passed the qualifications despite their uncertain origins. She will grow up without knowledge of her background unless otherwise specified by the HDPA or ACC. The HDPA or ACC will only resort to informing the half-demon of her background if it proves necessary to national security or the well-being of the majority of the populace. In accordance of Decree 24, she will only be used in matters regarding Xanedur, the half-demon's mother."

She read it over once, twice, three times, and then blankly stared at the page. Finally, she raised her eyes to meet Arabella's feeling confused at a sudden thought. "So the Prophet... said something that didn't make sense."

"Who?"

"The Prophet. The old lady that we were talking to this morning," Liz explained. At Arabella's expectant expression, Liz gave a quick glance to Liam to make sure he was still asleep. "She said that Liam was... more Chosen than me. Did you find anything on him that would explain that?"

Arabella shifted uncomfortably. "I did... But it's really weird, I mean... You're Chosen because you're a..." She trailed off.

Liz knew what she was going to say. "I'm a half-demon." She felt like throwing up after muttering the words.

"Yes. So one of your parents is a demon, but with Liam... Both of his parents are demons." Arabella paused for a moment and then stumbled on, "Your file was made by the Half-Demon Protection Agency, but it references the council my mother was on, the Alyspar Chosen Council – the ACC – and that's who made Liam's file, so I'm not really sure what that means."

"So wait –" Liz said, her eyebrows furrowing together as she tried to understand everything. "*Both* of his parents? Alina too?"

Arabella nodded. "It looks like, or at least she's a half-demon," she answered. Apologetically, she added, "I think it's best if he sees his own file first, but... I did find one on your brother." Liz felt a stirring of curiosity as well as discomfort. She was still trying to adjust to the idea of not being related to Alina or Liam. Plus it was hard to accept that she had a brother she'd never met and hadn't known about until that very morning. Arabella shuffled through the papers again and held one out. Liz took it, hands trembling.

Half-Demon Protection Agency
Person in Question: Levi Hart Kline
Cover: Michael Lee Marshall
Status: Cujan citizen
Father / status: Zachary Kline / Cujan citizen
Mother / status: Xanedur / demon
Sibling(s) / cover / status: Rachel Marie Kline / Elizabeth Jewel Prower / Alyspar citizen

"Levi Hart Kline, under the cover name Michael Lee Marshall, has been relocated from Avery, Cujan to Medo, Cujan. He will be placed with the Marshall family (Harold Wright Marshall / Julie Ann Marshall) and will grow up with limited knowledge of his background unless otherwise specified by the HDPA or CHDS. The CHDS has complete jurisdiction over which information is revealed to the half-demon, including but not limited to his own origin or his family members, including the demon Xanedur, the half-demon's birth mother. Due to Restriction 7, the half-demon will in no way be allowed to contact his sister, now Elizabeth Jewel Prower."

Liz tilted her head a little, looking at the pictures of her real brother. He looked familar with his dark hair, pale skin, and bright. blue eyes at age 15. But where had she seen him before? The doors flashed through her mind, and then she realized – he was the boy who had been in her dreams with Xanedur's Gate. He had said that Elizabeth Prower was only half of her... This is what he'd been talking about. She was half Elizabeth... and half demon. She had the sudden urge to go back to the doors to see him, to ask him all of the questions she had. Shaking her head, she rejected the idea. Those doors gave her an all new feeling of fear now that she knew what they were.

Looking up from the page with raised eyebrows, she slowly asked, "So my brother is in Cujan?" Arabella wordlessly nodded. "Are we going to meet him?"

"That's the plan," Arabella answered. A look of concern came over her face. "I'm just not sure if the Cujan authorities will allow it... But we're going to try. Maybe they'll let you stay with his family."

"I have nowhere else to go," Liz pointed out bitterly. As much as she yearned for her old life, with Alina and Liam, she still felt betrayed and confused. Alina had lied to her for her entire life. In the course of a single day, she had found out that Alina was not only unrelated to her, but was also a demon. If she was a demon, why hadn't she killed Liz? Weren't all demons inherently evil? Or were some of them good after all?

Trying to change the subject of her thoughts, Liz asked, "What's the CHDS?"

"I think it's the Cujan Half-Demon Society," Arabella said. When Liz remained silent, Arabella gave her a worried look. "Are you going to be okay?"

Liz absently nodded, murmuring, "Yeah. I just need some time to... think about all of this."

"I'll leave you to it then." Arabella's voice was quiet as she added, "I'm sorry to be the bearer of bad news... I'll tell Liam about everything when he wakes up." She held out a few more folded up papers for Liz to take, and with that, Arabella retired to the front of the boat, sharing soft words with Graham. He seemed tireless, expessing no interest in sleeping yet.

Liz looked at the papers Arabella had given her. They were research papers, all focused on the study of half-demons. Over the next day and a half, Liz read them each until she couldn't stop shaking. Her entire world... was crumbling.

How to Distinguish a Half-Demon.

Since the dawn of humankind, demons have been taking human form to engage in human activities commonly enjoyed as guilty pleasures, including but not limited to: sexual activities; gambling; and drinking.

Thousands of people have fallen victim to the flawlessness of the human form taken on by various demons, so it makes sense that there are so many half-demons walking amongst us today. But how do you tell if someone is a half-demon?

That's the thing – you can't. Only through careful lineage tracing can we determine whether or not demon blood runs through someone's veins. Half-demons inherit next to nothing from their demon parents – usually only physical characteristics of their human form.

Luckily for us, in modern times these things are traced by organizations such as the Half-Demon Protection Agency, an international group, or nation-specific groups such as the Alyspar Chosen Committee. These organizations commonly keep files on all known half-demons, also known as Chosen.

Unfortunately, there are unfiled half-demons who remain unaware of their parentage, or worse yet, were raised by demons masquerading as humans. These are the unknown Chosen who, though they have committed no direct crime on humanity, pose a serious threat to all of humankind.

Half-Demons and Their Uses.

Half-demons are considered by many to not only be half-demon, but also to have essentially no humanity left in them. However, there are various ways to use a half-demon to benefit humankind.

Though it is becoming a lost art in many countries, Alyspar still uses the sacrifice technique of expelling greater demons that have half-demon offspring. More often than not, their offspring are weaker and therefore easier to manipulate. The sacrifice technique works by taking a half-demon (or anyone with demon blood) to their demon descendant's Gate. A demon's Gate is where the Other World overlaps with our own world and is most commonly where a greater demon can be found.

Most techniques involve distracting the greater demon enough to sneak the half-demon into the Gate and then spilling a certain percentage (percentage currently unknown) of demon blood, which causes the greater demon to quickly deteriorate and eventually disappear altogether.

Queen Isabella

Regarding the children of Xanedur, we believe that it would be most beneficial to split them between our countries. How you handle your Chosen is under your jurisdiction, but Cujan has begun some intensive research on the Other World, and our efforts will continue to be largely funded until we've completely separated ourselves from the sacrifice technique. We will create their files with the HDPA and let you finalize Rachel's to fit your policies. Details of her journey to the border will be worked out over the next phone conference.

-*Cujan Half-Demon Society.*

"*Queen Isabella,*

We, as representatives of Cujan, wish to make clear our position on your barbaric practices of sacrifice as a means of expelling greater demons. We do not wish to start a war or damage relations between our two countries, but unfortunately unless you stop this injustice, we are afraid that we will have to cease our trade agreements and we will be in a state of hostility.

Our scientists are developing new methods of battling the demon race in less destructive ways and are more than willing to share our findings with your government and aid in future research.

-*Cujan Cabinet.*

Chapter 13

ARABELLA SAT NEXT TO LIZ AS THE SUN WAS SETTING ON THE second day at sea. Liz, having just finished reading the second letter to Queen Isabella from the Cujan Cabinet, written ten years after the first one from the Cujan Half-Demon Society, didn't look at her.

"These were all in your mom's room?" Liz asked numbly.

A sympathetic look came into Arabella's eyes. "Yes. They were in a safe. I didn't have much time, so I read through a few of them and snatched the ones having to do with the Chosen." Liz appreciated that Arabella had said Chosen rather than half-demon and finally met her eyes, trying to give her a reassuring smile. It felt more like a grimace.

"Does Liam want to see these?" she asked.

"I'm not sure," Arabella answered, casting a quick glance

over at Liam. He stood at the front of the boat with Graham, who was trying to teach him how to work the boat. Arabella looked back at Liz. "Are you doing okay?"

"I guess so..." Liz answered slowly. "I've stopped shaking at least." She held out a steady hand.

"Did you read them all?"

"Yes. I almost wish I hadn't."

"I hate my mother." A hard look came into Arabella's eyes as she looked forward. "I hate her."

Liz felt angry tears building up in her eyes at the mention of Queen Isabella. Her attempted smile vanished. "Were you going to let her sacrifice me?" she demanded, sounding a little harsher than she'd meant to. Arabella looked away and didn't answer for a while.

"For as long as I can remember..." Arabella began. "My mother was trying to get me on board with the whole sacrifice idea. Once, she had a big argument with Thomas. She revoked his right to the crown and planned on giving it to me instead – before they made up. That was the first time she showed me where she kept the Chosen." She winced at some hidden memories. "I can't forget the screams. I never liked what she was doing. I know that doesn't justify all of the lives I...I let her take, but...when you and Liam came along...I couldn't sit by anymore and do nothing." Arabella shivered.

Still resentful, Liz looked away, trying to hide a single tear rolling down her cheek. "So how many people know about the sacrifices?"

The fury in Arabella's eyes intensified. "My mother and

the rest of the Alyspar Chosen Committee. They're the ones who decide which Chosen need to go to Aloria, and they're the ones who kept the files and research all secret," she spat. "All of the researchers who wrote those papers are part of the committee. They've never even tried anything other than sacrificing innocent lives. Everywhere else doesn't even still do that. Then they try to hide it when demons start causing trouble so people don't think about it. Cujan is the leading researcher in using magic against greater demons rather than sacrifices, and they offered to help Alyspar, but my mother and the rest of the committee are too stubborn to accept any help."

They sat in silence for a while, both absorbed by their own thoughts. Eventually, Liam turned away from the boat's controls and walked back to join them with a sigh. As he sat next to Liz, Arabella awkwardly stood and said, "I'll go keep Graham some company. He needs someone to keep him awake."

Liz and Liam glanced at each other, their eyes meeting for an instant, before Liz turned her face away from him. About a week ago, things had been simple. She'd known everyone around her, and now suddenly she was surrounded by strangers, including the boy she'd thought was her brother.

"Liz, you can't ignore me forever," Liam pointed out, his voice quiet.

"I'm not ignoring you."

"You haven't even looked at me since we talked to the Prophet." Realizing that he was right, Liz sighed and shifted to look at him. He continued, "I just don't understand why

153

things have to change."

"You're not my brother," Liz said simply.

"So what?" Liam replied, sounding desperate. Liz didn't answer him, now looking forward instead of at who she'd once thought was her brother. In a few seconds, he added in a slightly irritated voice, "You're not the only one affected by this, you know. My mom is a half-demon, and my dad is a full demon. What does that make me?"

A freak, Liz thought, but she chose not to say it. In the back of her mind, she was aware that her bitterness shouldn't be directed at Liam. It wasn't his fault that she'd been lied to her entire life. Instead of commenting, she shrugged.

Liam looked at the open ocean surrounding them, his eyes distant. "I always thought I was special, but then I thought I wasn't when we got to Aloria. Then... I found out that I'm part demon. Our... *My* mom might still be alive... You think demons would have killed her?" He stopped, and when he went on, his voice sounded strained. "This isn't easy on me, you know. I'm mostly demon. At least you're half human."

Liz whirled on him, eyebrows raised. "Excuse me?" She looked at him with eyes like ice. "You think this is *easy* on me? You think I don't care that they were going to *kill* me? This is way harder on me than it is on you!" Suddenly she realized that she'd raised her voice and that both Arabella and Graham were looking back at them, startled. Lowering her voice again, Liz hissed, "I'm only half human, and that's enough of a curse to make my life hell."

Standing up, she stormed to the other side of the boat and

sat down again, glaring at the water with an ugly snarl on her face. Needing to do something as a distraction from Liam and his ignorance, she ripped out the last sheet of paper she hadn't looked at yet.

It was simply a map of the continent. Alyspar to the south, Cujan to the north. It was labeled "Names and Locations of Dangerous Demons in Alyspar and Cujan". To the southwest was the Alorian Peninsula, on which Koln wasn't marked. Of course it wasn't – it wasn't on many maps. Now, it wouldn't ever be on any maps again.

The Southern Peaks separated the peninsula from the rest of Alyspar, and the Alorian Bay was just north of that. The border between Alyspar and Cujan was visible, as well as a sizeable forest that dominated the northern half of Cujan. A small dot not far from the border had the name Medo over it, catching Liz's attention. That was where her brother – her real brother – was.

The Alysparian Desert took up the central part of the continent, ending at the mountains of the Middle Range to the east. In the very northeast corner of the continent, on the Alysparian Peninsula, were the Dry Mountains. The name Xanedur was penciled in over the mountains. Liz's anger immediately turned to an icy feeling at the sight of her birth mother's name. More demon names were scattered about the map, but Liz didn't recognize any of them. There were none on the Alorian Peninsula near Koln.

Putting the map away again, Liz shivered and wrapped her arms around her shoulders, though she didn't feel cold. After her heated conversation with Liam, a million thoughts were going through her head, some of which she wished she'd said.

At least you knew your mom. At least they didn't need to use you to kill her.

"Liz," Liam's quiet voice drifted to her from across the boat. "Please just talk to me."

Casting irritated eyes on him, Liz snapped, "Fine. What do you want to talk about?"

"Look..." Liam said, taking a tentative step toward her. "I'm sorry about what I said. You thought I was your older brother. Well, I thought you were my little sister. I thought our – *my* dad died on a hunting trip. But Arabella says he's alive, and my mom might be too." After a moment, he gently added, "I'm not the one they're after. When we get to Cujan, I'm taking the next boat back, and I'm going to find my mom and dad."

Mutinously, Liz mumbled, "You still want to see her after she lied to us for our entire lives? Because if I could, I would totally punch her in the face right now."

After that, they didn't speak. Liam looked down with an unreadable expression while Liz gazed haughtily to the shore, tracing its outline not too far away. Then her eyes caught sight of something on the water, coming closer at a fast pace. Alarmed, she glanced at Arabella and Graham, who hadn't seemed to notice it yet.

She was about to warn them when a sharp, male voice ordered, "Stop your engines!" A boat was approaching from the open ocean, and the thing Liz had seen was another boat coming from the shore. Their boats were bigger than the one Liz was on, casting a shadow that covered their entire vessel.

Arabella looked around in surprise, and then her voice drifted back to Liz, saying, "Graham, turn off the engine." The engine stopped, and Liz stood up, instinctively moving closer to Arabella and Graham. Looking closer at the boats, Liz saw writing on their sides: Cujan Sea Border Patrol.

The man who'd spoken before spoke again, pointing a gun at them warningly. "Put your hands in the air and state your identities and your business in Cujan waters!" He didn't seem friendly. In fact, he seemed rather unfriendly. Her feelings of anger forgotten, Liz moved even closer to Arabella and Graham, Liam right next to her. Arabella and Graham raised their hands into the air. Liz, heart pounding, copied them, seeing Liam do the same out of the corner of her eye.

Liz could feel herself trembling. In contrast, Arabella seemed confident as she called out, "I am Princess Arabella of Alyspar. I have with me one of Alyspar's Chosen and two of my friends. Please, we have nowhere to go. Let us speak to... whoever's in charge." Her voice tapered off at the end uncertainly, the only evidence of her fear. The man didn't lower his gun.

"What reason do you have to be fleeing your homeland?" he demanded. Arabella stared unwaveringly at him, straight into the face of a man completely prepared to shoot her. Liz, on the other hand, was trying to avoid looking at the gun, instead studying the other people on the boats, the boats themselves, and even trying to count the hairs on Arabella's head.

Anything that wasn't looking down the barrel of a gun.

Arabella said clearly, "I have sensitive information for the Cujan authorities. Queen Isabella is still sacrificing Chosen and was going to sacrifice her – " she glanced at Liz, " – but we escaped." The man shifted but did not lower his gun. He narrowed his eyes, considering them. His eyes were too small for his head, which looked quite bulbous. It wouldn't have looked quite so big if he'd only had some hair. He spoke over his shoulder, his voice too low for them to hear, and a bulky woman approached from behind him.

The woman said, "I'm boarding your boat, and we will accompany you to the nearest shipyard. You can use the phone there to speak directly to whoever wants to be the one to tell you to turn around and go home." Liz stared hard at the woman, trying to tell if she was serious. They couldn't go back. The woman stepped across the gap between their boats, which had lessened over time. Her bald colleague followed her along with two others. "Start the boat," she ordered. She seemed very comfortable with giving orders.

Graham was watching Arabella, clearly waiting for her decision. She nodded at him, and he left to start the boat again. One of the Cujanites followed him closely. Arabella made to join them, but one of the Cujanites stepped in her way. "You three are staying back here with us."

Liam, looking like he was about to faint, sat down as far away as possible from the Cujanites. Their faces were drawn in frowns. Liz shrank away from them, feeling exposed and endangered somehow. She wasn't sure what she'd expected, but it had definitely been more friendly than this. From Arabella's wide eyes, Liz guessed that she'd expected a warmer welcome too. The woman in charge was standing over Arabella, who looked her straight in the eyes defiantly, attempting to hide her fear.

For a moment, the woman looked furious that a mere teenager was challenging her authoritative manner. The boats began to move, two flanking theirs with another in front. The woman narrowed her eyes. After a few tense moments, during which Liz held her breath, the irritation left the woman's face, and the corners of her mouth lifted. She extended a hand.

"I am Captain Sasha. You are in our custody now. Trying to escape could be punishable by death or imprisonment. Pleased to make your acquaintance, Princess Arabella." The Captain gave a curt nod and looked out over the water toward the shore. Arabella seemed startled by the Captain's sudden change in demeanor, exchanging wide eyes with Liz. Glancing to the side, Liz saw that Liam was pale, almost looking sick.

An eternity of awkward silence seemed to pass by the time they reached the shipyard. From the back of the boat, with her eyes glued to Captain Sasha, Liz didn't realize that they were near the shore until a huge outgoing ship towered above them. Large ships all around them were still, docked and intimidating. Many were military ships, but a fair percentage of them were cargo ships or domestic cruise liners.

Catching sight of Liam's scared expression, Sasha let out a

snort. "Haven't you ever seen a cruise ship, kid?" she asked. Liam's eyes flicked to her face and then down to the pistol at her hip. He seemed paralyzed by fear. Sasha rolled her eyes scornfully and went back to surveying their surroundings, apparently confident that they weren't going to stage a revolt when they got to shore.

As soon as they'd docked, they were surrounded by more people with guns, all pointed straight at them. Arabella, shivering slightly, stared them down with a fierce look, though she cooperated as the Cujanite military members steered her, Liz, Liam, and Graham off of the boat. Something cold pressed into Liz's back, and she yelped in surprise. An arm kept her from turning around, but when she looked over her shoulder, it was the bald man, holding a pistol up to Liz's back. The others were receiving similar treatment as they were escorted along a path that led to a large building.

When they reached the building and were finally released, Arabella was the first to speak directly to the Captain, her voice shaking. "That boat, um… It needs to get back sometime." While her voice trembled, she showed no other signs of fear, boldly returning the hard look Sasha gave her. At last, Sasha nodded.

They were led into a small interrogation room inside the building, accompanied by a few soldiers and the Captain. Once they were all seated, the soldiers standing behind Captain Sasha, she spoke. "Now which one of you wants to explain why you're here?" she asked, glaring suspiciously at each of them in turn. Liz's stomach was doing flips. She looked down. In the corner of her eye she could see Liam and Graham also avoiding eye contact with the Captain. Arabella nervously tapped her foot. Sasha's gaze finally rested on Arabella. "You're the Princess, and you seem to be leading this troupe. How about you?"

"Okay..." Arabella mumbled, raising her eyes to meet the Captain's. Her composure broke for a second, and her voice cracked as she said, "The Queen of Alyspar was going to take Elizabeth away and sacrifice her. She's been lying to every country, saying that Alyspar doesn't use the sacrifice technique anymore, but she doesn't care about the Chosen. Please, you can't send us back," Arabella pleaded. "If we go back, she'll kill us all! We have nowhere else to go." Glancing up, Liz saw that Arabella was tearing up, though she refused to let herself cry. She was just as terrified as the rest of them.

Captain Sasha's eyes softened, and she spoke over her shoulder to the soldiers, "Resume your regular duties." Without a word, the soldiers left, and Sasha studied Arabella for a few moments, weighing her words. "Let's start with who you are. You said that you're the Princess," Sasha said, looking at Arabella. "But what about the rest of you?" She expectantly turned her eyes to Graham.

He spoke in a small voice, "I'm Graham. I'm... I was training to join the Royal Guard."

Nodding, Sasha said, "On to the next then." When Liz tried to speak, a small squeak came out. Immediately she could feel her cheeks growing hot, and beads of sweat were forming on her forehead. Sasha sighed. "Come on, we don't have all day. You don't need to be afraid of me. I'm only here to relay the information back to my superiors."

"E – Elizabeth," Liz stammered, her voice shaking. Sasha continued to stare at her. After a few moments, Liz finally added, "I'm Chosen."

Her gaze thoughtful, Sasha commented, "Ah, so you're the Chosen. Afraid that doesn't mean much here, kid. What about you?" Liz felt her entire body relax as the Captain's eyes moved away from her and on to Liam.

"I'm a nobody," Liam answered softly, his eyes looking downward.

"Ridiculous. Tell me who you are and why you're here," Sasha snapped.

"My name is Liam," Liam said, looking up with a determined expression. "And I want to go back."

Chapter 14

ARABELLA STRAIGHTENED UP AND STARED AT LIAM, her fear replaced by shock. "You can't go back! She'll kill you!"

"Why?" Liam shot back, glaring at her around Liz's head. "She didn't even want me at the Palace, why would she care what I do?"

"You're with us!" Arabella argued. "Graham and I would be charged for treason, and so could you just for being associated with us!" She turned to Sasha with pleading eyes. "You can't let him go, she *will* kill him."

"As I've said," Sasha said sternly, "you are all in my custody. Liam, until I've spoken with the Cabinet, I cannot allow you to leave. Any of you, for that matter." At Liam's outraged look, she added, "Cujan's national security is my first priority. It comes before anything else, including you." He looked back down at his knees with a sullen face. The Captain turned her eyes over to Arabella. "You seem to speak for your group. Would you mind explaining exactly why you could be charged for treason in Alyspar?"

Arabella seemed to weigh her words for a moment, her body tense. Then, sighing, she reached into her pockets and took out several of the different official documents she'd stolen from Queen Isabella. "Liz, do you still have the ones I gave you? Thank you," she said as Liz wordlessly handed them over. "Okay..." Arabella paused as though deciding where to start. "For one thing, we hurt some Royal Guards when we escaped from the capital. We broke into the Queen's room and stole these files, and we stole a car when we left. But the main reason is that we helped one of the Chosen escape alive and left the country."

Sasha raised her eyebrows. "Normally I would tell you to turn around and go home, but I think given teh circumstances of your... escape... you should speak directly with the Cabinet. Cujan doesn't support the sacrifice of innocents to slay greater demons, and any information you might have would be useful." Her eyes narrowed. "I would not be surprised if this leads to a war," she added darkly before leaving the room.

"War?" Graham echoed once she was gone. "But – why..."

"This is serious," Arabella told him quietly. "There are a lot of letters signed by my mother to Cujan's Cabinet that the sacrifices have stopped, but she's been doing just that all along. She's lied to the entire world about it for over ten years.

The rest of the world isn't going to just sit back and let her do that."

"You knew it might come to this?" Graham demanded.

"Well, I knew they wouldn't be happy."

Meanwhile, Liam was studying the others with a thoughtful expression. It made Liz uncomfortable; he looked almost like a cat preparing to jump on a mouse. Liz tried to shake off her discomfort and listened to Arabella and Graham speaking to each other in hushed voices.

Arabella was saying, "We're safe now. I hope I never have to see my mother again."

"I hope my family's okay..." Graham murmured. "My brothers would have to fight if it came to a war."

"And my mother would just sit behind a bunch of walls," Arabella said bitterly. "Hopefully Cujan will put her in her place before a war breaks out." She gave a sympathetic look to Graham. "I'm sure they'll be okay. They're pretty young to be drafted."

Graham glanced at her gratefully. "Whatever happens, I'm glad you're not involved in it anymore." His voice was soft.

"I'm glad you're not, too."

The door opened, and Sasha walked in with two guards behind her. "We're going to escort you to the capital so you may speak with the Cabinet in person," she informed them. "First you must go through the screening process for security purposes, and then we'll set out at dawn. Any questions?"

There was a moment of silence during which Liz felt the butterflies in her stomach turn into a hollow pit. Now that they were staying in Cujan, away from Queen Isabella, she finally felt safe. But after everything she'd been through on the way, she couldn't will herself to feel relieved or happy yet. Sasha nodded curtly and beckoned for them to follow her.

"Don't worry," she said. "At this point, the screening process is just a formality."

With Liz at her side, Sasha led them toward the barracks. She gave Liz a sideways glance and murmured, "I understand you and the Princess, but why the other two?"

Liz remained silent, looking at the ground in front of her feet. Her head ached as if a knife was driving through her skull. Eventually Sasha looked away from her, not speaking another word.

Suddenly, Liz felt too exhausted to think. She didn't comprehend where they went or what happened during the screening process. All she knew was that, now that they were in Cujan and being taken care of, her life was finally saved. Arabella hadn't been lying or trying to trick her, and she was now out of the Queen's reach. When she laid down to sleep, she fell asleep almost instantly, and she slept hard.

Surrounded by a deep blackness, Liz started to panic. Although she was moving her legs, she couldn't tell if she was actually covering any ground or if she was simply floating in oblivion. Was she dead somehow? Finally, something rose in the distance, and she desperately ran toward it. She stopped short when she saw that it was the doors. Xanedur's Gate.

They trembled and squeaked. Liz felt drawn to them, but

she resisted the urge to walk forward. A wisp of darkness waited as the doors opened, twitching to and fro behind them as if somehow impatient. Liz looked side to side for the stairs to get away, but she couldn't move. Once the doors opened, the wisp sprang forward, wrapping itself around Liz. Frozen by fear, Liz stood motionless, watching the darkness. Then it suddenly rushed to a spot in front of Liz and began to solidify into something.

There stood a pale woman with pitch-black hair. Her eyes were icy with cold pleasure at the sight of Liz, making Liz inwardly shiver. She didn't know for sure who this woman was, but she had a hunch.

"I've been looking for you, my child," the woman spoke. Her voice was low and silky. Liz stared at her with wide eyes, her blood running cold. "It's about time you've made it here. Any idea where your brother is?"

Shaking, Liz lied, "No..." She took a step backward, away from the woman.

The woman shrugged. "Pity. It would have spared you more time." Too scared to speak, Liz dumbly stared at her. The longer she looked at her, the more she felt like she was looking in a mirror. She inwardly shivered. The woman watched Liz thoughtfully for a few moments and then asked, "Do you know who I am?"

"I hope not," Liz answered, her voice sounding small and quiet.

The woman narrowed her eyes with a smirk. "Well, I may as well tell you that I am your birth mother. My name is

Xanedur." She tilted her head a bit, studying Liz. "I have been looking for you for a very long time. For some reason, I could not sense your energy on this plane, but then just a few nights ago, I heard you outside my very doors." She glanced lovingly at the doors over her shoulder, then turned a cold gaze onto Liz. "How I wished to see you so many years ago, make sure you were safe and happy. Then I found out that they were planning on using you to banish me from your world. It's too late now. The doors have opened. After tonight, I know where you are in your world. Your presence on this plane may not be strong enough for me to harm you here – yet – but your physical body is still within my reach." Xanedur's body faded, replaced by black mist, which seeped back through the doors.

Before the doors closed, Xanedur's whispered words drifted back to Liz. "May my love be with you, my daughter."

The woman shrugged. "Pity. It would have spared you more time." Staying silent, Liz just stared at her. The longer she looked at her, the more she felt like she was looking in a mirror, disturbing her even further. The woman watched Liz thoughtfully for a few moments and then asked, "Do you know who I am?"

"I hope not," Liz answered, her voice sounding small and quiet.

The woman narrowed her eyes with a smirk. "Well, I may as well tell you that I am your birth mother. My name is Xanedur." She tilted her head a bit, and then she added, "I have been looking for you for a very long time. For some reason,

I could not sense your energy on this plane, but then just a few nights ago, I heard you just outside my very doors." She glanced lovingly at the doors behind her. Turning a cold gaze back onto Liz, she whispered, "How I wished to see you so many years ago, make sure you were safe and happy. Then I found out that they were planning on using you to banish me from your world. It's too late now. The doors have opened. After tonight, I know where you are. Your presence on this plane may not be strong enough for me to harm you – yet – but your physical body is still within my reach." Xanedur's body turned to black mist again and seeped back through the doors.

Before the doors closed, Xanedur's voice drifted to Liz. "May my love be with you, my daughter."

Disturbed by her dream in which her mother had threatened her, Liz was barely able to think the next morning. Arabella caught her eye as they were walking to the cars that would take them through Medo and to the capital of Cujan, Knire. Knire was located just north of the Middle Range and Alysparian Desert, about halfway between the northern coastline and the mountains.

Arabella was sitting next to Liz in the car – a sleek, black sudan, driven by Sasha – and leaned toward her. "What's wrong?" she whispered.

Liz shifted. She looked at the rebel Princess, hesitant to speak about Xanedur and the things she'd said. But looking into Arabella's hazel eyes, she saw nothing but concern, and she realized how close she already felt to her. Suddenly, the thought of confiding in someone didn't seem so bad. "I...I dreamed about my mom – Xanedur, I mean – last night."

Quietly, Arabella asked, "You mean like a nightmare?"

Liz, almost imperceptibly, shook her head with a grim smile, turning her eyes to her knees. "That's not all," she went on. "I don't... think it was really a dream. It felt so...She said that my physical body is still within her reach," she finished, stumbling over her words. Her whole body tingled with discomfort.

Arabella's eyes grew wide. "What does that mean? She knows where you are?"

"She said she did," Liz answered, lip trembling. Now, more than ever, she wanted to forget all of this demon and Chosen stuff, and she wanted to go back to her old life. With all that was happening, she felt like her head was constantly spinning. Every morning she woke up, she was still shocked to find herself somewhere other than her bedroom back in Koln – which was now probably burned to the ground...

Arabella had been looking at nothing in particular, processing what Liz had said. "So... she's coming for you?"

Liz shivered. "I guess so."

They traveled in a small caravan of three government cars, each identical to one another. In the first car were military soldiers for their protection. Sasha, Liz, Liam, Arabella, and Graham rode in the second one, with more soldiers taking up the rear in the third car. Suspicious, as one would expect a Captain in the military to be, Sasha was sure that Queen Isabella would send Alysparian soldiers to retrieve Liz and the others. Graham kept reassuring them that there was no way the Queen would know where they'd gone, but Sasha still had her doubts.

As they made their way further inland, it was quite apparent that Cujan was more industrious than southern Alyspar. Most places south of Aloria had no paved roads, thus it was still necessary to travel on horseback. It was only near the capital city and in the surrounding areas that seemed to utilize modern technology. However, it appeared that Cujan was covered with roads; in fact, cars driving past them showed that plenty of people had cars to drive on these roads.

Medo wasn't far from the border with Alyspar, and it was near the coast where they'd been picked up. Liz was acutely aware that they would be passing through Medo, the city where her real brother, Michael, lived. She wanted to ask Sasha about him, but the remaining apprehension from her dream made her mouth feel so dry that she couldn't bring herself to speak. She figured that it would be pointless to ask anyway, as Sasha had not mentioned him before. Thus, it seemed unlikely that Liz and he would cross paths.

The car ride was uneventful and silent, everyone sticking to their own thoughts. Arabella had drifted into sleep, her head falling onto Graham's shoulder. Blushing slightly, he looked the other way, but he didn't wake her. Liz, with no distractions, kept imagining Xanedur and the Gate, just as she had been all day.

Having fallen asleep without meaning to, Liz found herself waking up as they slowed down. They'd reached the city limits of Medo. It was significantly smaller than Aloria, smaller than Liz had expected. But, as all places were, it was still quite a big larger than Koln. Many of the buildings were two or three stories tall, and the streets reached into the distance as far as Liz could see. The residential area they were driving through was cleaner than the lower district in Aloria. With the sun setting, there were still a few children playing outside and people walking about. They drove through downtown, flashing lights and signs too bright for Liz's tired eyes to look at directly. Her eyelids drooping, she hardly noticed when they'd entered another residential area.

"We're stopping right up here for the night, at one of our Chosens' safehouses," Sasha informed them.

Looking around at the houses, Liz couldn't see any that stuck out to her. "Chosens'...safehouses?"

"Your brother's residence," Sasha answered with a glance back at her. Liz suddenly felt very awake, butterflies fluttering in her stomach at the thought of meeting her brother in person rather than in her dreams. She almost didn't hear Sasha when she added, "It is a trusted residence, and we can't have anyone from Alyspar finding us if they try to track you down."

"Wait, wait," Liz stammered. "What is this about safehouses and trusted residences? Why are we...?"

"We can't risk staying somewhere public." Sasha paused for a moment, and then her eyes flickered as she realized how little Liz knew. "Cujan, unlike Alyspar, tells their Chosen about their heritage when they're deemed old enough

172

to know. We treat their residences as safehouses, top secret safehouses, where the Chosen can live safely while they learn dark magic. Dark magic is illegal to the average citizen. But since the Chosen are the only ones strong enough to use it against greater demons, they learn it in secret, partly so they can defend themselves... and partly so they can help us fight against greater demons."

A twinge of fear shadowed Liz's nervousness as Arabella sat up, blinking sleep from her eyes. Seeming to only have heard about the possibility of Alysparians following them, she asked, "You think Alysparians might know where we are?"

"We don't want to make any assumptions," Sasha said firmly. "But we can't be too careful. You're safe now, but if they find out that we're protecting you... Well, based on what you've said, I'm sure it would lead to a war between Cujan and Alyspar." Liam opened his mouth to say something, alarmed, but before he could speak, Sasha said with a note of finality, "No more questions. We're here."

She pulled the car over, parking along the street. Liz's stomach was churning, threatening to make her throw up. She'd been looking forward to this moment for only a few days, but she'd longed for it so heavily that it felt like she'd anticipated meeting her brother for years. The dreams in which she'd met him seemed far away, now that it was about to happen for real.

Liz couldn't feel her own legs or feet as they walked up the pathway, and Sasha knocked on the door. The windows of the houses around them were lit up, illuminating the street around them, with the sky finally growing dark. Liz saw a shadow move in the window, a face briefly peeking outside, then it disappeared. A moment later, the door opened. A tall boy stood there, looking just as he had in Liz's dreams. He smiled, appraising them. "Hello," his somehow familiar voice said. "I'm Michael."

Chapter 15

LIZ STARED AT HER BROTHER IN WONDER. THIS WAS IT. This was the moment she'd been waiting for. He looked exactly as he had in their shared dreams.

He looked at her past Sasha, curiosity gleaming in his eyes. With a curt nod at Sasha, he said, "We've been expecting you. Glad you got here safely."

Sasha nodded back at him, then nodded to the soldiers, waiting out next to the government cars. One of them raised his hand and flicked his fingers back to the cars. After they'd all gotten in, they drove off.

"Where are they going?" Graham asked, looking after where the cars had disappeared from view.

"There is no room for them all to stay here. They are heading to nearby safehouses," Sasha answered him before turning her eyes back to Michael. "It was an easy drive, no problems at all. Let's go inside. We'll do introductions once we're out of sight."

The house was clean and nice, with pictures of Michael as he'd grown up along the walls. Liz looked at them as they walked past, comparing them to him as he led them forward. She wondered when they had told him the truth. How had he reacted to it? Had he lashed out at everyone like she had?

"Okay," Sasha's voice broke Liz from her thoughts. They'd reached a spacious living room with an open layout, an island the only thing between the living room and the kitchen. "Michael," Sasha said, "this is Arabella, former Princess of Alyspar." Michael bowed his head to her respectfully. Looking embarrassed, Arabella glanced away. "This is Graham," Sasha went on, gesturing to Graham as he stood awkwardly by Arabella's side. "This is Liam. And this... This is Elizabeth." Michael met her eyes, and Liz's insides first seemed to bunch up together. But as she returned her real brother's gaze, her anxiety melted into a strange feeling of... safety. Security. Even so, when she first tried to speak, her voice seemed stuck in her throat.

"C – call me Liz," she stammered.

"It's a pleasure to meet you, Liz," Michael said warmly. He tilted his head slightly to the side. "I'd always wondered if I'd get to meet my sister."

I'd always thought that I already knew my brother, Liz thought, but she kept the thought to herself.

Sasha beckoned to Michael, and the two of them moved

off to the side, leaving the four friends alone. Liz stared after Michael until Arabella tapped her shoulder, and the four of them formed a small circle. Arabella's eyes were shining.

"This is perfect," she whispered. "Liz... Your brother..." Arabella was breathless, looking over her shoulder at Michael. "He needs to come with us."

Liz tilted her head questioningly.

"For one thing," Arabella explained, "he can explain to you more than the files show. For another... If he comes with us to the Cabinet, he can help our case. They trust him."

Sasha and Michael talking where Liz couldn't hear them made her insides churn with discomfort. What if they were plotting against them? But at the same time, she felt like she was walking on air after finally seeing him in person. "We can ask Sasha, can't we?" she asked. Arabella and Graham nodded approvingly.

"I like him," Graham said quietly. "I think we can trust him." Liz didn't know why exactly, but she agreed with him.

Sasha and Michael came back to stand beside them, and they broke their circle. Sasha gave them a curious look, a question in her eyes. Then, dismissing it, she gestured farther inside the house, saying, "Michael will show you to your rooms. We leave at ten in the morning. I think we can all use a good night's rest." And with that, she left them, going up a flight of stairs off to the side that Liz hadn't noticed at first.

Michael's eyes were friendly as he invited them to follow him down another hallway. "My parents are asleep, but don't worry. I'll take good care of you all." He left Arabella,

Graham, and Liam in different rooms, leaving Liz alone with him.

"Big house, huh?" she commented, wanting to break the silence but not knowing what to say.

Michael glanced over his shoulder at her. "My mom is the CEO of R&M."

"R&M?"

"Right and Might. It's a clothing company here. I forgot they don't have any stores in Alyspar."

"Oh."

"We had a smaller house when I was younger, but... After they told me who I was, we had to move to a bigger house. At that point, they were turning our house into a Chosen safe-house, so we needed one with lots of spare rooms. Liz, has our mother ever opened the doors to you?"

His question caught Liz off guard, and she winced. He obviously noticed, because his eyes narrowed and a strange look came into his eyes. Liz tried to recover, but she could only stare at him for a few moments before she let out a breath. The memory of Xanedur saying that Liz's physical body was still within her reach in mind, she answered slowly, "Yes... Why?"

Michael's face fell. He solemnly said, "You're in great danger then. We have to talk about this tomorrow, okay? Don't let her open the Gate. We can't let her know where we are." With that, he turned and started to walk away. Pausing, he looked over his shoulder one more time. "It's nice to finally meet you."

Liz couldn't get the image of the doors out of her head. She didn't know how she was supposed to keep the Gate from opening. The voice of her mother was in her ears as she fell asleep.

Dreamless sleep granted Liz her first restful night in a long time, and she woke up feeling rather refreshed. For a moment, everything felt unreal, and she just stared at the ceiling, wondering if it was all a dream, and she'd wake up at any moment. But she blinked again and again, and the white ceiling didn't go away. Eventually, she got up and wandered to the living room.

Everyone else was already there, sitting and chatting with one another. After she'd fled from Koln and then the capital of Alyspar, it felt strange to see these people having normal conversations and laughing, as if there weren't demons and Queen Isabella to worry about. She felt close to Arabella and Graham, grateful for their part in getting her away from Aloria and the Queen's grasp. Even Michael, after meeting him in dreams and finally in person, seemed like someone she could trust. If she hadn't developed those relationships with those three, she may have been bothered by the sudden distance from Liam. But with new friendships and a new family of sorts, she hardly noticed his glare at her as she sat down. No one else seemed to notice her at first.

Then Michael met her eyes and smiled. "There she is," he announced. Everyone's eyes turned on her; Arabella and Graham grinning; Sasha's default military-grade cool shadowed by fondness; Liam's resentful gaze, with something else behind it she couldn't read; and then the two strangers she'd noticed as soon as she sat down. They were a middle-aged man and woman, whom Liz could only assume were Michael's parents. She looked at them, they looked back with curious eyes. Michael stood up and walked to Liz's side, facing his parents.

"Mom, Dad," he said, "this is my sister, Elizabeth. Liz, these are my parents."

"Call me Harold," the man said, reaching out a hand. As Liz took it, he added, "It's very nice to meet you, Elizabeth."

"I'm Julie." The woman smiled, also shaking Liz's hand with a soft smile. "We've always hoped to meet you one day."

After the introductions, they all resumed casual conversations. Liz's nerves, which had tightened up her chest for a few moments, calmed again. She felt lighter than she had in what seemed like a long time, for once not running without looking over her shoulder. They were safe, here with Captain Sasha and hidden where the Queen wouldn't find them. Michael beckoned to her to speak in private. The sounds of laughter fading behind her, she followed him into the hallway.

"Last night," he spoke with a serious expression, "you said that Xanedur had opened the doors to you. When did she do that?"

The light feeling in Liz's heart dropped like a heavy weight. "Well…" She thought hard, but she wasn't sure which dreams had just been dreams. Maybe, she hoped in vain, she hadn't really seen Xanedur. Maybe it had just been a freak nightmare.

But at the same time…

"She would have spoken to you," Michael pressed, his voice low and his eyes intensely searching hers.

"A couple of nights ago," she finally answered reluctantly. She had just woken up; she didn't want to think about demons and her birth mother.

Michael contemplated her response for a few tense moments, staring off at nothing. "We have to get you out of here then," he said. "We have to get you somewhere she won't find you. Once we get to the Cabinet, we'll be safe for a while. Once they find out that Xanedur's trying to find you, they'll take care of everything. They'll keep you safe."

"How?" Liz whimpered, feeling worlds away already from the laughter floating to them from the living room.

"I forgot that Alyspar… does things differently than Cujan," Michael responded dryly. "Cujan doesn't sacrifice their Chosen. Instead, once the Chosen reach a certain age, they take them to a special academy over in Knire." Knire, Liz recalled, was the capital of Cujan. "There, they teach the Chosen how to control dark magic to use against greater demons."

"Dark magic?" Liz repeated. "They have you *use* dark magic? Against greater demons?"

"The Chosen are better at using dark magic than other people," Michael explained, speaking quickly, reminding Liz that their time was limited. "Not only that…" he added, more slowly. "Without demon blood, when people go near a greater demon's Gate, they get really weak. It saps the life out of them, makes them unable to move even. The Chosen, though... The Chosen are able to move around and everything without being slowed down like most people. When you have demon blood in your veins, that doesn't affect you."

"So Cujan uses its Chosen as part of an army against greater demons?" Liz asked, trying to process the new information.

"Basically, yes."

"What about you, then?"

"I know some dark magic. I haven't had to use it yet, but... part of being Chosen means that you have to take on some responsibility."

She stared at him. "But it's not our fault that we're... half-demons." The words felt like acid slipping on her tongue.

"Sometimes you have to accept that while something's not your fault, you're the only one who can help fix everything."

Liz didn't believe a word of that. She didn't *ask* to be Chosen. She didn't want to be in this mess.

Lost in her thoughts, she almost didn't hear Michael when he sighed, "We'd better get back to everyone. We need to leave, get you out of here as soon as we can. She didn't visit you last night, did she?"

Liz shook her head absently.

"Good."

They rejoined everyone in the living room. Sasha looked around, making sure everyone was present, before standing up with a grim smile. "We should be going," she said, glancing at the large clock on the wall. It was almost ten, just when they'd planned to leave. Before she could say more, Michael pulled the Captain off to the side, whispering urgently into her ear. Her eyes grew wide. Liz exchanged a tense glance with Arabella as Sasha called Harold and Julie over as well. The four of them spoke together for several seconds. Michael said something, to which Sasha shook her head firmly. Then Harold and Julie spoke, and Sasha closed her eyes while they grew silent. She turned to Liz and the others.

"Michael is coming with us," she announced, sounding defeated. Michael looked at Liz with glowing eyes and walked over to her, Arabella, and Graham. Liam was standing off to the side, observing them all through thoughtful eyes. Sasha, Harold, and Julie continued to speak. Liz overheard some quiet words, "… she knows… we'll have to move … not a safehouse anymore…"

Then Michael was with them. Arabella and Graham watched on as Liz asked, "What did you say to her?"

"My parents and I have to move again, if Xanedur knows where we are." At their confused looks, he added, "If she knows where you are, then she knows where I am. It's too risky to stay here any longer. My parents will move while I stay with you guys and Sasha, for my own safety." He rolled his eyes at the last part.

"Oh no," Liz said, covering her mouth with her hands. "It's my fault…"

"No, no," Michael chided. "Alyspar didn't tell you anything about any of this. They should have, but they didn't. It's not your fault they're stuck in their old ways. Anyway…" A sly smile formed on his face. "I wanted to go with you guys."

Arabella spoke for the first time, "Why are you really

coming with us then?"

Michael gave a steady look at Liz. "I'm the only one who can keep her safe from Xanedur. Sasha's an old family friend, and she knows a lot about the Chosen and everything, but even she doesn't know everything I've learned about being Chosen in disguise. No one does." Arabella exchanged a glance with Graham and nodded.

"We'd been hoping that you would explain some things to us," Arabella admitted. "We were planning on asking Sasha if you could come, but we didn't really know how to go about it. You beat us to it, anyway."

Michael smiled. "It's probably for the best that I did. She's always been soft on me."

Liz hadn't noticed Liam sulking off to the side for a while now, but it looked like he'd moved closer to the front door, his eyes glued to Sasha and Michael's parents. Liz watched him carefully, elbowing Arabella for her attention. Before Arabella was even able to look over at him, Liam had stealthily opened the door and slipped through.

"Sasha!" Liz cried in alarm, suddenly realizing what was happening. She pointed to the door as Sasha swung around, her voice failing her.

Arabella, however, never at a loss for words, filled in for her. "Liam is leaving!"

Sasha bolted to the door, flinging it open and sprinting outside. Liz, Arabella, Graham, and Michael quickly followed her, Harold and Julie shadowing them. Liz got to the door just in time to see Liam shut himself into the driver's seat of the car.

The engine started as Sasah reached the doors, but the car was locked. As she raised an arm, about to punch an elbow through the window, the car violently lurched forward, throwing her off onto the ground. And with that, Liam was speeding away, running into a garbage bin. It fell to the ground, spilling its contents. Sasha looked after him and then to her immediate surroundings, desperately searching for something, anything, to stop him with, but before she could find anything, he was gone, taking a corner too fast and running over a curb. The sound of the tires squealing quickly faded into the distance.

"Where are the guards?" Arabella gasped as Sasha dejectedly walked back to them. "They could stop him-"

"They stayed at a hotel downtown. They've already left to return to their station," Sasha answered blankly. "From here on, we were going with minimal security to attract less attention. I can't believe I trusted that kid." She listlessly shook her head, eyes empty, as she entered the house.

Chapter 16

LIAM HAD STOLEN THEIR ONLY CAR. AFTER SASHA HAD contacted the guards, still at the hotel they'd stayed at the night before, all they could do was wait. There was no chance of them catching Liam now. They sat in the living room, no longer laughing or joking. It was silent, and the air felt heavy and stuffy as if all of the air had settled in the middle of the room.

After what felt like much too long, Michael spoke. "Why would he leave? Where's he going?"

"He's going back to Alyspar," Liz answered darkly. "He hasn't been the same since he – since we found out he's..." She broke off, her voice cracking with emotion.

"His dad was a demon," Arabella said for her hollowly. "His mom was a half-demon. He grew up thinking that Liz was his sister."

"He's going back to find them," Liz spat, her sorrow turning into anger as she thought about it. "He always wanted to be… special somehow. Guess he got what he wanted."

They sat in silence for a while longer before the two sleek, black cars pulled up to the curb. When the guards heard that Liam had taken the other car, they shared uncomfortable looks. They seemed unconvinced that he was going to find his parents. One of them murmured to Sasha, "What if he goes to the Queen, ma'am?"

Sasha looked away and didn't answer him.

With some of the guards staying behind at Michael's house for the time being, they piled into the two cars. Three guards were going with Sasha, Liz, Arabella, Graham, and Michael, making a total of eight. Sasha, used to thinking like a soldier, wanted to keep them all with her in case something happened; the three guards followed them in the other car. Liz sat in front with Michael, Arabella, and Graham in the back. They were silent, each to their own thoughts.

Liz's mind was preoccupied with Liam's sudden departure. Was he going to Queen Isabella? They had only just gotten away from Alyspar and the Queen's terrible clutches. Liz didn't want to have anything to do with the situation anymore, content to stick wherever she was safe in Cujan.

"Where do *you* think he went?" Sasha asked Liz quietly. "You know him better than any of us."

Liz didn't look at the Captain, instead gazing distantly out the window. "I'm sure he's going to find his parents," she lied, her voice slow. Even though she'd been feeling very far from Liam, she still knew him well enough to know that he would go to the Queen. What he would reveal to her though, Liz wasn't sure. She tried to dedicate her thoughts to other things.

Closer now to Knire, the capital, they'd stopped for another night in a small town along the road. "We should get to Knire the day after tomorrow," Sasha told them before leaving them to their rooms in the hotel. Their guards stayed stationed outside, trying to remain inconspicuous. Liz and Arabella were in one room with Michael and Graham in another.

When Liz and Arabella had settled in, Liz noticed that Arabella looked significantly more dejected than her usual bright self. "Arabella," Liz said carefully, "what's wrong?"

Arabella jumped out of her thoughts and met Liz's eyes. "Liam is going to be killed over there, I just know it. I can't believe he ran off like that. And... Never mind," she finished quickly, looking away.

Liz narrowed her eyes suspiciously. "You can tell me what's bothering you. We're friends, aren't we?" she pointed out.

A small, half-hearted smile formed on Arabella's face, and she gratefully moved her eyes back to Liz. "Yeah, we are. I've never really had any friends except for Graham." Arabella paused, and her smile faded. "I'm just thinking... What are we going to do after we get to the Cabinet? Graham and me, I mean."

Dumbly, Liz blinked at her. She hadn't even thought about

what would happen after they got to the Cabinet. Instead, her mind had been trained on self-pity having to do with the current situation. The idea of what they would all do after they'd explained their case to the Cabinet hadn't even crossed her mind. "Maybe they'll put you somewhere safe?" She started to feel more worried as she realized that she didn't even know what would happen to herself.

"They wouldn't send us back, would they?" Arabella asked desperately, dark memories swimming in her eyes.

"No," Liz replied instantly, though she didn't know that for sure. "I'm sure they won't send you back." After a few moments, during which they both looked down at the floor, Liz slowly said, "Maybe... we just need to focus on what's going on now. We can figure that out when we get to it, can't we?"

Arabella silently nodded, though she didn't seem convinced. After a while, they took their places in their separate beds, and Liz quickly fell asleep.

Liz was surrounded by a fine, dark mist at first, stumbling over ground she couldn't see. Soft voices seemed to be speaking around her, but she couldn't understand what they were saying. Breathing heavily, she suddenly burst out of the the mist and let out a grateful sigh. Then she saw the doors.

Just as tall and intimidating as ever, they stood open. Nothing moved inside. Liz held her breath, her eyes set on the darkness inside the doors. As she stood there, a marble balcony became apparent underneath her feet with stairs spiraling their way down a cave wall. The stairs went down into a black abyss.

After her last experience when the doors had opened, and with what Michael had said, Liz was sure that Xanedur would come out of the doors soon. Trying to be as quiet as possible, Liz began to move toward the stairs, every shred of her being telling her to get away, but her footsteps echoed against walls she couldn't see, making her wince with every step. With the marble balcony's smooth, tall rails preventing her from jumping, which she was desperate enough to do, the stairs were her only way away from the doors.

She had almost made it to the stairs when a soft voice drifted toward her from the doors. Chilling Liz's blood and making her tremble, it said, "So there you are."

When Liz had awoken, she was drenched in sweat, her heart pounding inside her chest. Arabella had just stood up and was looking at her with wide eyes. "Are you okay?"

Liz could feel herself visibly shaking. Meeting Arabella's concerned eyes, she whispered, "I don't think so."

After telling Michael about her dream, Liz's brother just stared at her. "You're not safe here. We have to go *now*." He spoke to Sasha in a low voice, and she turned to glance at Liz, alarmed. With a gesture toward the hotel entrance, she led them to the cars.

As they drove away from the small town, Michael talked to Liz in a quiet voice. "You saw the marble balcony?"

Liz nodded wordlessly.

"Then she knows exactly where you are. The more present

you are in that world, the more connection she has to the physical world."

"What do you mean by 'that world'?" Liz asked. "The dream world, you mean?"

"No, it's the world between this world and the Other World," Michael corrected her. "The Other World is the demons' realm. When your energy begins to cross into the Other World, you might experience one of those 'dreams'," he explained, "where you appear at the Gate. When you're there, if the Gate opens, the greater demon can sense your physical presence because of your energy crossing over."

Liz's eyebrows furrowed together as she tried to process what he was saying. "Why didn't the Gate open before now for me?" she asked.

Michael shrugged, answering thoughtfully, "It's possible that your energy wasn't present enough there for Xanedur to sense it. As you get older, your energy becomes more powerful. The Gate opened for me when I was fourteen."

"How do you know all of this?"

"Cujan's been researching this stuff for a long time now," Michael said. "Half-demons that are documented here are becoming more involved in the Cabinet's efforts to figure out how to locate and banish greater demons. By using half-demons' connections to their respective Gates, those who are trained in dark magic find out where Gates are and go destroy them."

"How do they find the Gates?"

"Like I said, half-demons use their connections to the

Gates. They focus their energy on that plane and figure out approximately where the physical Gate is, and then people trained in dark magic go find it and destroy it," Michael explained patiently.

Before they could speak more, the car lurched and threw them forward. Startled, they looked outside, trying to figure out if something had hit them. Sasha slammed on the brakes and drew a gun, ordering, "Stay here." She got out of the car. The guards behind them had also stopped, jumping out with guns raised. Liz watched them turn all around with a sinking feeling in her chest, searching for whatever had hit them.

With no warning, a shadow rose up behind Sasha and shoved her to the ground. Before they could react, more shadows came up and pulled the guards down as well. Then, the back car door was torn open, and the shadowy form of a demon looked in at them. With a scream, Liz forced the other door open, and they all piled out. Arabella, on the end where the door had been torn off, was snatched by the demon before she could get out.

"Where is the girl?" the demon growled, the other demons holding the guards on the ground. They were all helpless. Liz cowered on the other side of the car, hoping to stay out of sight. She was violently shaking, her feet frozen to the ground. Michael and Graham stood facing the demon. Michael looked petrified, but a furious light came on in Graham's eyes at the sight of Arabella being held hostage.

His voice trembled as he demanded, "Let her go!"

The demon let out a low cackle and tightened its grip on

Arabella, who was tensed up in shock. "Give us the girl!" the demon insisted viciously. Arabella let out a whimper as the demon further tightened its grip.

Liz stayed silent, feeling as though her lungs had collapsed and her heart had plummeted right out beneath her, though she could still feel it pounding harshly against her whole frame. Her vision swam with her pulse, her hands cold and clammy. Michael still looked to be in a terrified trance. Graham was the only one of them who moved forward.

"She's not the one you're looking for," he said in a dangerous voice. "Let her go."

"Not until you give us the girl! Give us the girl!"

Another demon, holding down an unconscious Sasha, spoke, "Unless that *is* the girl…"

The demons all let out chilling laughter that sounded like nails scraping against glass.

"That's not her!" Graham's voice sounded shrill now. The laughter seemed to have thrown off his courage as he shrank away a little from the demon holding Arabella. Arabella gulped and desperately looked at Liz. After a few heartbeats, the fear in her eyes dissolved, slowly replaced by determination.

"Stop trying to protect me, Graham," she said quietly with resolve. She took a deep breath and relaxed. "I am who you're looking for."

A wicked smile crossed the demon's face.

"Ara-"

Arabella spoke over Graham's protest. "Take me! Just

please don't hurt my friends."

"We don't care about them," the demon said as it began to melt into a liquid shadow, enveloping Arabella and streaking away across the ground. The others quickly followed suit. Liz caught one last glance of Arabella's terrified face as she was taken away, and then the demons were gone.

And so was she.

Chapter 17

FOR SEVERAL MOMENTS THEY WERE ALL SPEECHLESS. Sasha and the guards were still unconscious.

Then Graham broke the silence, growling, "We have to go after her."

"Are you crazy?" Liz shrieked. She felt like she was going to be sick. Graham stared at her in disbelief, but she hardly noticed. Her heart was pounding so hard she felt like it was going to break her ribcage open. She added, "She's probably dead already!"

Graham rounded on her with eyes like daggers. "It's *your* fault they took her in the first place!" he snarled furiously, making her take a frightened step back. "How could you just sit there and let them take her?"

"How could *you*?" Liz shot back. "It's pretty obvious how you feel about her!"

"I tried to stop them more than either of you did!" Graham shouted with an accusatory tone, casting a glare at Michael, who was standing silently to the side. "You were no help either!" They were quiet for a moment, and then Graham's eyes were back on Liz. "How could you let them take her?" he asked, his voice suddenly quiet. Tears were starting to form in his eyes. "She saved your life. She risked her own life for you, she gave up everything she had for you."

Liz fell down to her knees on the ground and tightly shut her eyes, trying not to let his words get to her. But in her head, she saw Arabella's scared eyes as the demon held her back. *She's dead,* Liz told herself. *She has to be dead. Demons don't take prisoners.*

"Demons don't take prisoners," she repeated her thought in a soft voice.

A tear escaped Graham's eye and slid down his cheek. "Why didn't they kill her right here then?" he asked, his voice shaking. "She's still alive. She has to be."

Liz opened her eyes but, though the ground met her gaze, still saw nothing. A part of her wanted to let Arabella take her place. Let her die as the demons' prisoner. Then this whole mess would be over.

But another part of her knew that Arabella was alive. That she would be taken to Xanedur, who would know that Arabella wasn't who she wanted. And Xanedur wouldn't stop until she had Liz. Whether they went after Arabella or not, Xanedur would find Liz, no matter where she went. The difference, then, was that if they didn't go after Arabella, she would die. And Arabella was innocent.

It was true that Arabella had given up her entire life of royalty to save Liz and Liam. And though Liam had run away, Liz was still in debt to the former Princess. With Arabella's face in her mind, she tuned back into the present, where Graham was speaking with Michael.

"You didn't do anything..."

"I'm sorry. I just – I've never..."

"I'm going after her."

"What, by yourself?"

"If I have to."

"No, you'll – you'll be killed! Not just anyone can defeat even a lesser demon, let alone a greater one!"

Graham turned dangerous eyes to Michael. "What about you? You were the one who wanted to come with us to protect Liz."

"I mean, I guess I... Yes." Michael paused.

"We're going after her then?" Graham asked seriously, hope beginning to sparkle in his eyes.

Michael nodded determinedly, seeming to surprise himself with the action. "You're not Chosen. You need someone who can get near the Gate."

Graham slowly looked at Liz. "Liz..." he murmured. "Are you with us or not?"

Liz stared at him and opened her mouth, but no words came out.

Michael turned on her, almost aggressively, a sudden hard look in his eyes. "Liz. What do you think the Cabinet's going to do? They'll debate about it for several days at least, then they'll send Chosen after Xanedur. At that point..." He looked away and blinked. "It will be too late to save Arabella. We might not be the best people to take on a greater demon by ourselves, but-" he looked between Graham and Liz, his head held high, "I think if anyone can do it... We can."

Liz blinked, inwardly groaning. All she wanted to do was hide behind the Cabinet, where she would be safe and maybe be able to forget about all of this. But Michael was right. The Cabinet wouldn't send anyone in time to save Arabella. She would be tortured until death claimed her. And if Liz decided not to go, they would leave without her, and she would be left here with Sasha and the guards, none of whom she was entirely comfortable with. She had only just met her real brother, who understood her and where she was coming from. She didn't want to lose him merely days after meeting him.

"I'm..." she whispered finally. "I'll go."

A hopeful glint rested in Graham's eyes. "When are we going?" he asked with a glance at Sasha and the guards.

To their alarm, Sasha let out a pained groan. "Going... where?" She was trying to sit up. Her eyes were on fire, but her body seemed unresponsive to her efforts. Looking over her shoulder, she turned her gaze onto each of them in turn. Panic flashed over her face. "Where is Arabella?"

Liz's heart plummeted as she helplessly stared at the Captain. Graham covered his face with his hands, his shoulders shivering in a silent sob. Michael was the first to speak. "They took her. The demons took her."

Sasha's eyes widened in disbelief. "No..." she gasped, forcing herself to a sitting position. Wincing, she raised her hands to her head and shut her eyes for a moment. Then she looked at them again. "Do you... Do you know where they took her?"

They exchanged glances among the three of them and looked back at Sasha again. Graham started to say, "We don't –" but Michael cut him off.

"Liz and I... Liz and I can find out."

Staring hard at him, Liz asked, "The Gate?" Michael nodded. Then Liz remembered the map Arabella had found with greater demons' locations labeled on it. "Actually..." she murmured, "we don't have to find anything out. I have a map that shows almost exactly where Xanedur's Gate is."

Sasha watched them carefully for a moment. Her gaze fell to the ground as she sighed. "I can't allow you to go after her."

"What?" Graham's voice was dangerously quiet, fire in his eyes. Sasha looked back up at him, seeming alarmed.

"I can't let you go after her," she repeated. "It's too danger-ous, and we can't afford to spare any more lives. Especially not yours. They've probably already killed her," she added bluntly. Liz, Michael, and Graham stared at her.

"If they were going to kill her, they would have done it right here!" Graham raised his voice angrily. "She's alive. What's wrong with you? She risked her life to get here, she doesn't deserve to be put through all of this!"

Sasha's voice became hard. "There's no way I'm allowing

you to try to save her yourself. We'll report it to the Cabinet, and they'll send some Chosen to go after her."

"No!" Graham protested. "*We're* going to save her!"

"Graham," Michael said patiently. "Maybe she's right." He gave Graham a weighted look. "Maybe we *should* let the Cabinet take care of it." He spoke slowly.

Graham blinked at him, stunned. Then a shimmer of understanding came into his eyes. "Whatever." He stormed off a little distance.

Liz looked between Michael and Sasha. But evidently, Sasha hadn't caught on to the message shared between Michael and Graham.

Their eyes all traveled in their own directions, their spoken words dissolving into thoughts.

"Liz."

A soft voice woke her from her slumber. She opened her eyes to see Michael standing over her, Graham a small distance away. It was dark.

After the demon attack, they'd been forced to camp out for the night while everyone recovered, both physically and mentally. Some of the soldiers, who hadn't ever seen a demon face to face, had looked at the ground with empty eyes that couldn't see until they'd fallen into an uneasy sleep. Liz, even though she'd been cornered by demons more than once now, was still shaking, despite having slept for a while.

Liz could barely recognize Michael with Graham standing behind him. "What is it?" she asked tiredly, trying to keep her eyes open.

"We need to talk," Michael answered, holding a finger up to his lips. "But quiet. We can't wake them." He nodded toward Sasha and the guards.

"What do we have to talk about?" Liz still felt too tired to think straight.

"Arabella."

That woke her up, the image of the demon ripping the car door open coming into her head. She silently followed Michael and Graham as they walked away from their camp. Once they were far away enough to not risk waking Sasha and the guards, Graham was the first to speak.

"We're going after her. Michael and I talked about it, and we're going, with or without the others. Arabella needs us. And I…" He didn't finish his sentence, but he didn't need to. Liz looked at Michael, waiting for his input. He looked back at her, determined.

"We're leaving tomorrow night. I checked a map, and that's probably when we'll be closest to Xanedur's Gate before the road goes north toward Knire. We'll have to go on foot though, some of the way will be off-road…" Michael paused. Then, "Are you sure you're coming with us?"

Liz hesitated. She was sore. Her feet hurt. And she was scared. But she wasn't sure what she was scared of more at this point. The idea of being left alone in an unfamiliar place with unfamiliar people on the way to the Cabinet, or the idea of going straight where Xanedur wanted her to go – to the Gate.

She didn't want to say no to her own brother, and Graham's desperate expression tugged at her heartstrings so much it hurt. Arabella had taken her place, sacrificed herself for Liz. She'd given up everything she had as the Princess of Alyspar to help Liz escape certain death. As much as Liz didn't want to put her own life at risk...

"I'm... I'm going with you," she said, looking at the ground. When her eyes traveled back upward, Michael gave her a grim smile. A flame of hope came into Graham's eyes.

"We'll leave once everyone's asleep tomorrow," Michael decided. "For now, get some sleep. I'm not sure how much we'll get on our way to the Gate."

"What if... What if she's not at the Gate?" Graham asked, his voice barely audible. He was staring into the distance, fear making his eyes wide. Michael and Liz exchanged a glance.

"It's the best idea we have right now. In any case, we need to get away from these guards first. Once we're gone, we can decide for sure where we're going." There was a note of finality to Michael's words. They dispersed and went back to sleep.

Liz had strange dreams that night. Or at least... she thought they were dreams at first.

A shrill scream cut through her head, and Arabella appeared, surrounded by darkness. The darkness evaporated to reveal a marble balcony - *the* marble balcony - inside of a cave with steps leading downward at least twenty feet to the ground. On the balcony, carved into the cave wall, were the doors. They were open.

Arabella was being held back by shadows on the balcony, struggling in vain to get away. The shadows slowly brought her closer to the doors – to Xanedur's Gate. Liz suddenly found herself on the uneven ground below the balcony, looking upward at Arabella as she was forced into the doors.

"Arabella!" Liz cried. Trembling violently, she started taking the steps two at a time, hoping to get to Arabella before the shadows took her completely. A cold voice made her freeze in her tracks, and Arabella's scream was cut off.

"Don't worry," the voice murmured. Xanedur, in her lithe human form, came out of the Gate and stood on the balcony, resting her arms casually on the railing. The doors swung closed with a loud thunk. "I won't have her killed yet," Xanedur went on. "You will come for her, I'm sure. She will be kept in the Other World near my Gate until then. I hope to see you soon, my daughter." Everything around Liz began to fade, and she plummeted into nothingness. When she awoke, she felt as if all of her breath had been stolen from her. Still shaking, she didn't speak a word to anyone while they ate a small breakfast.

They drove in silence. Arabella's absence was an unspoken disturbance to them all, Liz's dream fresh in her mind. She wanted to tell Graham and Michael about it so they would know that their plans to run away weren't in vain, and that she was being held at the Gate after all. But with Sasha there, Liz's tongue caught in her throat. So she, too, stayed quiet.

Liz watched as the sun rose. As the green grass turned to dark, sun-scorched dirt and sand, stretching as far as the eye could see. The Alysparian Desert. The sun went high in the sky. The air rippled with heat, causing the illusion of distant water on the ground. Hours went by. The dirt and sand combination turned to dirt and rock. Stunted bushes and dead trees grew scattered around the desert. Eventually, the jagged mountains of the Middle Range rose from the ground, far away. The desert reached all the way to the base of them, as far as Liz could tell. They would be approximately in the very middle of the continent by now. And to think that, by that night, they would be as close to the Dry Mountains on the Alysparian Peninsula as possible before the road would turn north toward Knire.

The sun finished its arc across the sky, painting dark colors across the sky. A jarring red that faded into a soft purple, which gradually turned to black. She found it more fitting to her mood than the blue sky of day.

The car stopped eventually, and they got out to set up camp again. Liz cast an apprehensive glance at Michael and Graham. They were setting up close together, so she joined them without a word. Sasha looked at them with pity in her eyes and didn't question them being so close together, a small distance from the rest of the camp.

Just after the fire had died out and they were getting ready to sleep, the heat of day finally fading, they heard vehicles approaching. Far down the road from the way they'd come, headlights shone. There were at least three cars, speeding down the road toward them.

"What in the world-" Sasha muttered, standing up to get a

better view. "They must be in an awful hurry…"

As the cars got closer, it became clear that they were not Cujan cars.

There was only one other place the cars could be from.

Sasha's eyes filled with panic as she tried to maintain a cool composure. "Michael, Graham, Liz, get out of sight. Now!" she snapped, trying to keep her voice steady.

They obeyed, hiding behind the nearest car. The incoming darkness helped to cover them from the Alysparians' sights.

The cars stopped, and several people, armed with guns, jumped out, immediately pointing their weapons at the Cujan party. "Where are the fugitives?" someone demanded.

"What fugitives?" Sasha asked, sounding calm. Without giving them time to answer, she said with authority, "I am Captain Sasha. You might want to take a look at a map and figure out which side of the border you're on before you start asking questions like that. And lower your weapons, for your own sakes. Who are you, and why are you here?" Liz admired the Captain's ability to stay composed with such a sensitive situation.

Unable to see from the other side of the car, Liz could only listen as the leader of the Alysparian party answered, "I am of the Royal Guard of Alyspar. We are here for our rightful prisoners, traitors of the Crown. Two young girls, one of whom is the former Princess, and an older boy. Names of Arabella, Elizabeth, and Graham."

"What makes you think they're with us?" Sasha demanded. Viciously, she added, "And for the gods' sakes, put down those guns! You have no right to point them at us as things stand."

"Intel says that they were last with a group of travelers on their way to see the Cabinet."

"And why did you believe this 'intel'?"

"Because it came from someone who was previously with the party, a previous enemy of the Crown. Thought to have been the brother of Elizabeth."

Struck by shock, Liz's head started spinning. Liam? *Liam* had gone back to Alyspar and told the Queen where they were? She was unable to breathe, unable to blink, unable to move. Michael and Graham were staring at her with wide eyes, but she couldn't look at either of them. She started to lose her balance, her vision swimming, crouching behind the car. She'd thought that she knew Liam like the back of her hand. She thought he'd have snuck into Alyspar and gone straight to the Alorian Peninsula to look for his parents. But instead… he'd gone to the Queen.

Not capable of stopping herself, she couldn't catch herself. In slow motion, she fell, Michael and Graham frantically trying to catch her before they lost their cover. But they were too slow. Liz fell to the ground away from the car and into the sight of the Alysparians.

Everyone was quiet for just a split second that seemed like an eternity to Liz. The Alysparian captain shouted, "There they are! Capture them alive! Lethal force on the others!"

The Alysparians hitched their guns back up and began to fire at the Cujan party. The Cujanites tried to pull their own firearms but most of them were too slow. Bodies fell like rag-dolls.

The shock of hitting the ground woke Liz from her trance-like state. Michael was suddenly pulling her up to her feet. She, Michael, and Graham were running from the site, some-how avoiding the bullets ricocheting off of the cars and flying through the air. One glance over her shoulder revealed to Liz that Sasha had been shot. She was on the ground, flat on her back, unmoving. And behind them was an Alysparian Royal Guard, chasing after them.

"Guys!" Liz screamed at Michael and Graham, picking her feet up faster. Michael looked back at her and saw the Alys-parian warrior. He paused, turning around to face the wom-an. Graham and Liz ran past him, Liz stumbling over the uneven ground. Her eyes were glued to her brother, alarmed. But, as Michael had said, he was proficient in magic.

A small, concentrated blast of darkness came from his hands, hitting the Alysparian square in the chest. She fell to the ground, apparently dead. Michael froze, his eyes wide. Liz stopped, staring between her brother and the dead body. Graham, however, was more able to move in dire situations. He skidded to a stop and raced back to Michael, shaking him by the shoulders.

"We have to move!"

They caught up to Liz. The Alysparians and the Cujanites were evenly matched. In the confusion, Liz, Michael, and Graham, managed to get away, fading into the night like si-lent shadows.

Chapter 18

THEY'D BEEN WALKING FOR HOURS. GRAHAM INSISTED
that they keep going through the night and wait until the
day to rest, wanting to get to Arabella as quickly as possible. Michael agreed with him for the sake of getting as far
away from the Alysparians and Cujanites as they could, and
so they wouldn't walk through the day's heat in the desert.
To Liz's relief, the sky was beginning to turn from black to
a dark purple, fading to a milky yellow hue on the horizon,
foreshadowing sunrise. Soon they would stop, and she could
finally rest.

Graham and Michael were walking close together, whispering to each other. Exhausted, but suspicious and curious,
Liz tried to sneak closer to hear what they were saying. Graham was asking, "Do you know where we are?"

Michael shook his head. "The mountains are this way.

When we stop, I'll try to direct my energy to find the Gate. I'm sure that she's there."

Remembering her dream, which she hadn't gotten the chance to mention yet, Liz spoke up. "She is at the Gate. I saw her."

Michael stopped short and gave her a worried look. She caught up to them, and he resumed walking, though he was considerably slower. "You were there? The doors were open?"

"Yeah. Xanedur... She told me that Arabella's there, in the Other World. She's keeping her alive."

"So she knows where we are?" Michael asked, alarmed.

"Yes," Liz answered carefully, "but she's waiting for us to go to the Gate."

Graham's eyes were sparkling with hope, relieved that Arabella was still alive and that they knew where she was. Michael, however, had a thoughtful frown on his face. Then he said decidedly, "So we're walking into a trap."

"A trap?" Graham echoed, sounding defensive. "Saving Arabella is a trap?"

"That's not what I meant," Michael answered dismissively. "Xanedur is waiting for us. She knows that we're coming, and she's ready for when we get there."

Liz's feet hesitated, and she stumbled forward. "What is she going to do when we get there?" she asked, her voice small. Graham glanced at Michael, waiting for an answer. He looked troubled, caught between the idea of rescuing Arabella and the thought of Xanedur's wrath when they got to the Gate.

Michael watched the ground as he walked, stepping over rocks and small bushes. They were approaching the Cujan-Alyspar border, east of the Alysparian Desert and Middle Range that dominated the center of the continent. They would have to push on through the remaining dry conditions, going along an old unpaved road that led to the next town on the border. After that, they would be entering the Dry Mountains, where Xanedur's Gate was located.

Finally, Michael answered her, but his words offered no comfort. "I don't know. I don't know what she'll do."

Liz knew he was lying.

"How do people even…find a Gate when they're asleep?" Liz asked Michael when they'd stopped walking. The peaks of the Dry Mountains were just barely on the horizon, the road they walked along old and riddled with weeds. The desert around them had patches of grass here and there, telling of the end of the Alysparian Desert. As the sun began to rise, Liz realized why they would want to walk at night. The temperature was already climbing. Her voice was scratchy, and her throat was dry from lack of water. They had nothing to eat, nothing to drink. Liz hoped that they reached the nearby town during their next period of walking so they could get some provisions. Otherwise, she didn't think she'd have the energy to make it to the Gate.

Michael sat on a flat rock and met her eyes. "I've almost found it before," he started as Graham joined him on the rock, a pained look in his eyes. Michael continued, "You focus your energy on the Gate when you get between here and the Other

World while falling asleep. I don't know if you know how to do that or not, but…" He trailed off, looking at Liz curiously.

She shifted uncomfortably, suddenly aware of just how much knowledge Alyspar had kept from her. "I have no idea."

"I'll try to do it today. I'm sure I'll fall asleep since I didn't sleep at all when we stopped before." Liz was acutely aware of the bags under her brother's eyes. "If you manage to do it, well…" he went on, "be careful. When you find the physical location of the Gate, the greater demon instantly knows exactly…*exactly*…where you are. Xanedur is going to know where we are, and I don't know what she'll do with that information."

"She wants us to go to the Gate…" Liz said slowly, her thoughts churning. Lack of sleep, food, and water was clawing at her mind, muddling her thoughts. "She's playing with us."

"What makes you say that?" Graham asked, yawning.

"She's holding Arabella captive, and she's waiting for us," Liz said with certainty. Michael and Graham looked at her and then at each other for a moment.

"It makes sense," Michael commented, though he sounded dubious. "We still have to be careful. Once she knows where we are, she might send demons after us to get you and me."

Graham's light snores drifted over to Liz as she laid on the ground, trying to fall asleep. Michael was silent, but she could tell that he was awake.

"Michael?" she whispered.

Michael immediately answered, "What's up?"

"Has Xanedur ever tried to capture you?"

Michael was quiet for a few seconds, and Liz thought that maybe he'd fallen asleep. Then he spoke, "She tried to when I was younger. The first time the Gate opened."

Liz stared up at the blue sky, the sun just above the horizon. Despite the calm tranquility of the landscape around them, she was overwhelmed by a sense of hopelessness. "What happened?"

"She just...sent demons after me. My whole family had to move. They'd put me with a family that knew all sorts of magic, even dark magic. That's the only reason I'm alive, because of them. It's illegal for everyone except the select few that devote themselves to fighting demons. My parents used to do that stuff."

"Why does dark magic matter?" Liz asked.

"It's the only magic that's truly effective against demons," Michael replied quietly. "It's the only magic we have that's of their world, the only thing that can truly destroy them." Moments passed where neither of them spoke. Then Michael patiently pointed out, "Liz, we need to sleep. We're almost to the mountains. We need to know where Xanedur's Gate is, and we need to sleep to find that out."

Liz nodded, though she knew he couldn't see it. "Okay. Good night. Or, I guess, good morning," she corrected herself.

"Good morning," Michael murmured, and eventually Liz's vision turned black, and she fell asleep.

The first thing Liz noticed was how cold she was. Her skin

felt like it was pressed against ice, and for a moment, as a brisk breeze blew over her, she forgot how to breathe. She couldn't tell if her eyes were open or closed because all she saw was darkness everywhere she tried to look. She was trying to move, but it felt like she was suspended in this darkness. Eventually, a gray mist began to seep around her, and that's when she knew that her eyes were open.

She heard a loud clang, and finally she found that her body responded, so she spun around. The doors stood before her, as intimidating as they always were. Covered in those deep green vines with roses sprouting out at irregular intervals, they stood still and silent. The roses, which had been red and vibrant, shriveled up, their color fading to a dull gray. A strong wind picked up, pulling the dead roses from the vines and whipping Liz's hair into her face. Still the doors stayed silent.

Liz's feet felt unnaturally cold. Looking down, she saw that her feet were bare, flat on the marble balcony. To her right, there were stairs that ran down the moist wall of a cave. Slowly, her eyes traveled down the steps, expecting to see mist eventually like she always did. But this time, the steps kept going.

They stretched all the way down to a dirt floor. A strong, musky odor hit her, the smell of earth. Holding her breath, Liz looked down over the rail of the balcony. It was a shallow cave, the end opposite the balcony not far away. Liz looked to her right, away from the walls of the cave. A distance away, she could see a cloudy sky and huge, rocky mountains.

Sunlight from behind the clouds poured into the cave. Liz glanced back at the doors, but they still hadn't opened. Shaking with nerves, she took a step toward the stairs, then hesitated. Another fearful look at the doors showed that they hadn't opened still. She felt like if she moved too much, they *would* open, and she would see Xanedur again. But as she took another tentative step, they remained silent and closed.

Slowly, Liz put her foot on the first, cold step and continued down the stairs.

When she'd reached the cave floor, the doors still hadn't moved, so she kept walking toward the cave opening. It was cold, and she shivered, realizing that direct sunlight couldn't have ever hit the inside of this cave. The pungent odor of earth faded the closer she got to the opening until she was standing in dim sunlight. She shielded her eyes; after having been in the dark cave, even the sunlight from behind the clouds was too bright.

As her eyes adjusted, she saw that she was surrounded by mountains. The cave with the doors itself was carved out of the side of a mountain. Suddenly, Liz gasped as the sensation of being outside of her own body came over her. Her vision, fast as lightning, jumped away from her body and traveled upward into the sky, looking down at the ground.

She saw the vast valley the cave was in, and then she was too far away to pick it out as she went up and over the tops of the mountains. More and more mountains appeared, getting smaller the higher she went. Then she could see all of the mountains in the entire range, and she realized that she was looking down on the Dry Mountains. But she didn't stop there.

Liz kept going up and up until she could see most of eastern Cujan and Alyspar, including the Alysparian Desert, which was like a huge, brown scar just to the west of the Middle Range. Somehow, she felt a connection between the cave she'd left behind and the spot she, Graham, and Michael were in, and she had a clear sense of where to go to find Xanedur's Gate. With another sharp gasp, she was back in her own body in the valley.

Spinning around to look at the cave, Liz could barely see the doors in the darkness. A deep boom issued from inside the cave, and the doors started to open. With black mist seeping out from behind them, Liz heard a blood-curdling scream – Arabella's scream.

Breathing hard, Liz's eyes snapped open. The sky was clear and bright above her. She hastily scrambled to her feet. Michael and Graham were both looking at her with alarmed expressions.

"Liz, you okay?" Michael asked. "You seemed like you were having a nightmare. I was just about to wake you."

"I saw – I had – the Gate –" she mumbled, unable to speak coherently, staring at them with wide eyes.

A look of awe came over Michael's face. "You saw where the Gate is."

Liz nodded, shivering at the memory. "Has that ever happened to you before?" she demanded.

"No. I've never located the Gate before. What was it like?"

215

Michael asked excitedly. Graham looked between the two of them with confused eyes.

Liz breathed, "It was unbelievable! I was at the Gate, like usual, and then – then I saw mountains, I saw outside the cave, so I walked out, and then…it was like I was outside of my own body, I flew up into the air and saw everything, the entire continent…" She trailed off, breathless.

Graham spoke up for the first time, "So does that mean you know where Arabella is?"

Liz met his eyes, still unable to speak clearly. "Yes, it does."

The sun was getting close to setting. Without food or much water for the last day and a half, Liz felt weak, and her throat was parched. The hot sun beating down on them wasn't helping anything. The ground here, save for the abandoned road, was largely dark sand with scarce grass. The sand made walking difficult, and it got in Liz's shoes. But she didn't want to be the one to stop them when Graham and Michael were determined to keep moving. The longer they took to get to Xanedur's Gate, the more she would suffer. Time was of the essence.

Finally, Michael stopped, wiping sweat off of his forehead. "We should rest for a while. Liz, how much longer will it take for us to get there, if you have any idea?"

Liz looked up, her breath ragged. "Another day maybe?" Her voice was quiet.

Michael nodded slowly, closing his eyes as he thought about something. Graham's eyes hovered on Michael for a few moments, then he walked a little distance away, sitting down on a rock. Liz sighed in relief. She was tired, and she didn't want to walk anymore. Her feet had still been aching from the walk from Koln to Aloria. There were blisers all over her feet by now, she was sure, so every step was painful.

Some time passed. The sun was casting red light far across the sky, meeting a deep blue and purple on the opposite horizon. Liz had given up on avoiding the sand and laid down, trying to ignore the uncomfortable feeling of sand in her dark hair. Eventually, unable to sleep, she sat up and looked around for Michael and Graham. Michael was seemingly asleep on the sand, facing away from them. Graham was still sitting on his rock, staring at the sunset.

Liz approached him. "Can I join you?" she asked politely. Graham nodded, his eyes glued to the sunset. He scooted over on his rock a bit to make room for her. She sat next to him and followed his intense gaze.

After a while, Graham spoke. "Arabella loves sunsets. She likes to say that the sun is painting the sky before it goes to sleep."

Neither of them said anything for a long time. The sun disappeared behind the horizon, and the sky faded to violet and black. Gradually, a rumbling noise sounded in the distance. Liz didn't think much of it at first, hardly noticing it, but then it started to get louder. It was impossible to see much in the twilight, so she couldn't tell for sure what was making the noise. But it sounded a lot like approaching cars.

Liz and Graham stood up and looked at Michael, eyes wide. Liz's brother had already sat up and was intently staring into the darkness, back on the road. Suddenly, he blinked and jumped to his feet.

"Run," he told them, ushering them in front of himself.

"Who is it?" Liz yelped, almost tripping on the loose sand.

"I don't know who it is for sure," Michael answered as they picked up speed, "but they have cars that look an awful lot like the Alysparians'."

"Have they seen us?" Graham demanded, looking back toward the cars for a second. Liz glanced over her shoulder too and vaguely saw the cars driving along the road in their direction.

"I don't think so," Michael said. "We have to get off the road and find a place to hide, before they..."

As he spoke, the cars' engines revved. They were speeding up, crashing over the sandy rock.

"They've seen us!" Liz shrieked in a panic. She, Graham, and Michael stumbled over the ground. To Liz, it seemed hopeless to try to escape. They were already weak from not eating and dehydrated from lack of water. She could feel her entire body screaming in protest, not running in a straight line.

Without warning, Michael stopped, his feet kicking up sand. "Wait!"

"What are you doing?" Graham cried. "We have to go, let's go!"

Michael gave him a significant look. "If we let them capture us, they'll probably take us to the Gate."

Liz's heart fluttered in her chest. "To sacrifice me to

Xanedur."

"Yeah, or they'll take us back to Alyspar and kill us!" Graham argued.

"They wouldn't do that to Liz."

"Michael –" she started to say, but he cut her off.

"We won't let them take us all the way there. I won't let them give you up to Xanedur," he promised, looking her straight in the eye.

"Michael, this is too risky!" Graham insisted. "We have to –"

"Too late," Liz interrupted him, slowly turning back with a sinking feeling. The cars – there were two, large off-road vehicles – had stopped, and the Alysparians were getting out with raised guns.

"Stop right there!" a man commanded.

"We're already stopped," Graham pointed out quietly.

The man glared at him. "No talking! You're all coming with us." He approached them, not lowering his gun, and jerked his head for two others to follow him. The three only holstered their guns when they reached Liz, Graham, and Michael. The man who'd spoken roughly pulled Liz's arms behind her back and shoved her toward the cars. "We're taking you to the Gate, and we're doing what should have been done as soon as you made it to Aloria."

Liz, Graham, and Michael didn't say anything as they were forced into a car, but Michael gave Liz a reassuring look. The cars began to move. Liz felt like she was going to throw up.

On one hand, they were going to get to Arabella that much

faster. On the other, they were once again being held captive by Alysparians. And if they weren't careful, Liz would be sacrificed to Xanedur.

Chapter 19

WITH THE CARS, IT HADN'T TAKEN THEM LONG TO REACH a paved road that would lead them to a small town, Fore, at the base of the Dry Mountains. They were closer to Xanedur's Gate than ever before. Liz had stayed silent as ordered, trying to shut out the image of the doors. She was terrified of facing Xanedur at last.

Michael sat quietly next to her, Graham on his other side. None of them spoke. The two Alysparians in the front of the car didn't even look at them. There was a taut mesh barrier between the front and back seats, not allowing those in the back to reach those in the front.

The sun was rising, painting the sky a milky yellow. They'd been driving all night. Liz peeked around the seats, trying to see if the small town of Fore was on the horizon yet. Apprehension made her heart split in two, half of it soaring upwards and the other half falling like lead in her stomach. Lights shone from up ahead, but there were dark, Rocky Mountains looming not much farther than that. Xanedur's Gate wasn't far now. Liz could feel it.

"We're stopping here," one of the Alysparians said. His tone offered no room for a response.

When they stopped, the Alysparians got out, leaving Liz, Graham, and Michael trapped in the car. They disappeared into a small hotel.

"So what's the plan?" Graham asked immediately. Liz carefully tugged at the door handle, but the door didn't budge. Michael frowned.

"Well…" he said carefully. "Should have known that would be too easy." He looked hard at the hotel doors, a thoughtful expression on his face.

Liz nervously looked back at the second car, where other Alysparian guards waited. "We have to get out today," Liz told Michael in a low voice. "We're too close to the Gate. A couple more hours of driving is all it would take."

"And if they got us there themselves…" Michael murmured, "well… we'd be in trouble then."

"They'll probably try to separate us," Graham pointed out. "What will we do if that happens?"

"We'll have to make a run for it before they can," Michael said decisively. He started talking faster, his eyes trained on the hotel entrance, where the two Alysparians were coming back out. "You two just follow my lead. Liz, you're going to have to hit hard."

Before Liz could ask what he meant, the Alysparians had opened the car doors, suspicion in their eyes.

"Let's go," the driver ordered.

The next morning, it was early enough that the hotel was still serving breakfast. The Alysparians brought Liz, Graham, and Michael into the breakfast room, keeping their heads low. Graham and Michael walked close to Liz. Michael whispered, "They must not want Cujan to know that Alysparians are here, or that they have Chosen with them."

"We can use that to our advantage," Graham whispered back. Liz said nothing, unsure of what else to add. She nervously watched the people mill about as they ate. The smell of bagels, toast, eggs, and hash browns hit her all at once, and her mouth started to water.

The Alysparian driver said quietly to them, "We have our eyes on you. Get some food, sit down, and stay quiet. Otherwise, we'll kill you right here, right now." To show that he meant what he said, he lifted his shirt just enough to show the holstered gun at his side.

Liz's appetite hesitated, her entire body suddenly feeling very cold. But once the driver had walked away to sit in a corner with the other Alysparians, she could feel hunger gnawing its way through her stomach. Her throat felt like the sandy desert they'd been walking in. Graham and Michael led the way to the food, looking equally as hungry.

As they walked, Michael spoke quietly. "Okay, so we're going to get food first. We'll need our strength to get to the

Gate. Liz, how long will it take us to get there on foot?"

Liz closed her eyes for a moment and felt for the path they would need to take. "It's not far into the mountains," she answered confidently. "We could be there by sundown if we left now."

Michael and Graham exchanged a glance before the three of them sat down to eat. Liz couldn't recall having ever felt this hungry in her life. Her stomach had felt like it was caving in, and now that she had food again, it felt like her stomach was too small.

Graham saw her hastily shoveling a waffle into her mouth. "Careful," he warned. "You don't want to eat more than your stomach can handle." Liz paused for a moment, and then she began eating more slowly. He was right. If they were going to run for it, she didn't want to do it on a more-than-full stomach.

Almost immediately after they'd finished their food, the Alysparians were there. "Get up. We're taking you to your rooms to prepare for our departure." Michael snuck a glance around them as they got to their feet. The room was still crowded. The Alysparians pushed them toward the door, and once they were close –

Michael shoved one of the six Alysparians into another hotel guest. Not even a second later, Graham had forced another one of them onto the floor, hard. Liz dumbly stood with wide eyes at the unfolding scene. Before the Alysparian could turn around to threaten Michael for pushing him, the hotel guest he'd run into – a large, burly man – turned around and glared at him. Then a look of understanding came into his eyes.

"You," his tone was hostile, "are from Alyspar." Without another word, he punched the Alysparian in the face, knocking him out completely. The one Graham had shoved had fallen to the floor, other guests staring down at him and trying to help him up. He was surrounded and unable to join the other four Alysparians, who were advancing rather quickly on Liz, Graham, and Michael. One lunged toward Liz, but before he reached her, Michael jumped in the way, wrestling with the Alysparian.

"A little help, Liz!" Michael grunted as he threw the Alysparian into the crowd of hotel guests. Another Alysparian, about to reach Michael from behind, suddenly fell sideways to the floor, stunned. Liz's fist was out, and she realized that she'd punched the Alysparian, apparently hard. Taken aback, she blinked, staring at the unmoving Alysparian on the floor. Michael pulled at her, saying something, but she couldn't hear anything around her. The whole world had gone silent.

Behind Michael, Graham jabbed a punch to one of the Alysparians' gut, and the Alysparian - a small-framed but strong woman - flinched. In that time, Graham grabbed her and threw her into the last Alysparian, bowling them both over. The crowd around them was panicking now, pushing past each other to try to get out of the room. The Alysparians, trying to get back up, kept being shoved back down to the floor in the crowd's frenzy. Graham led Michael, with Liz in tow, with the flow of the crowd, rushing out of the breakfast room and into the hall. They jumped out of the crowd and into the lobby, sprinting for the doors.

As Liz's hearing returned, she briefly heard the hotel desk attendant exclaim, "Excuse me, what's going on?"

Then Liz comprehended the words being exchanged between Graham and Michael. "Is she okay?" Graham was asking.

"I think so – just shocked," Michael replied, not breaking stride.

"I'm okay," Liz told them too loudly. Michael nodded as they ran, and he let go of her, getting in front of Graham.

Liz's knees felt weak, but she couldn't let Michael and Graham – and Arabella – down, and she didn't want to be left behind to an uncertain fate. She continued to run behind them, struggling to keep up. They took a sharp right and went around the hotel, down a busy street. It was early enough that people were rushing to work, congesting the sidewalks. To avoid them, Michael turned again, taking them down a shaded alleyway and away from the hotel. As they turned the corner, Liz glanced over her shoulder to see two of the Alysparians just as they spotted her. She ran faster.

"They're coming!" she cried to Graham and Michael. Michael quickened their pace even more.

Liz felt like her lungs were going to burst already, but she pushed onward, following Graham and her brother onto another busy street. They took a left, pushing their way through the crowd. Cars were driving back and forth, pushing out fumes. Michael cast a glance behind them and gestured to the street, making his way in front of oncoming cars, seemingly without fear.

The closest car, just feet away, skidded to a stop, and a loud honk issued from it. The driver leaned out of his window, yelling, "Hey, watch it!" Another car suddenly stopped as the driver realized that they were running across the street, and the car behind it rammed into its rear bumper, causing a loud crash. The Alysparians, still on the chase, tried to rush the street too, but the first Alysparian was struck by a car, rolling up and over the top, and finally landed on his back on the ground. The second Alysparian took one more long look at Liz, Graham, and Michael, but she stopped beside her comrade, halting the oncoming cars. Liz looked back at her brother, her head throbbing.

With the Alysparians momentarily distracted, the trio left the town of Fore behind. Michael led them, a little slower now, toward the Dry Mountains.

"Why didn't we grab one of their cars?" Liz asked wearily. She hadn't meant for it to sound like a whine. But the blisters on her feet made every step more painful than the last, a constant reminder that she'd been on the run for, well... a while now.

They were hiking down the side of the rolling hills that stood between Fore and the tall peaks of the mountains. Once they reached the mountains proper, they would be in Alyspar again, on the Alysparian Peninsula.

"Does it look like the cars would do us much good here?"

Michael pointed out, looking at the empty land surrounding them. It wasn't as hot as the desert had been, and with the food they'd eaten, their energy and strength had been restored. They'd left the road behind and were now traveling cross-country to avoid the Alysparians, should they continue their chase. It was also the quickest route to Xanedur's Gate.

Michael stopped and stood there silently for a moment before saying, "This is about where the border with Alyspar is. I've never been out of Cujan before."

"So what?" Graham asked impatiently. He'd been seeming more agitated by the minute the closer they got to the Gate. "Arabella's in Alyspar, so that's where we need to go."

Michael shook his head, almost in a sad way. "Maybe you should take the lead now, Liz," he suggested. "You know where the Gate is better than I do."

They made their way up and down more hills that steadily got steeper and steeper until they were not rolling hills but instead mountains jutting out from the ground. Their path was a series of low points between the mountains, the particular zig-zag route of which was hidden to all but those who knew the exact location of Xanedur's Gate.

Liz was already out of breath as they were gaining altitude. She knew exactly where they needed to go and how far away it was. It wasn't an easy path – and the Gate wasn't far.

Chapter 20

THE GATE WASN'T FAR INTO THE MOUNTAINS. THEY'D finally come to a vast valley, where Liz suddenly stopped and stared ahead with wide eyes without seeing anything. They weren't far from Xanedur and the Gate, and the thought of facing her mother in the flesh was hitting Liz at last.

"Liz?" Michael prompted, coming up to stand by her side. "What is it?"

Without looking at him, she responded, "We're here."

Graham came up on her other side and looked into the valley. "Are you sure? Where is it?"

Liz pointed to a rocky outcrop on the far side of the valley. "It's hidden over there. You can't see it until you get close."

"Graham..." Michael began cautiously. "Maybe it's best if you wait here while Liz and I go get Arabella." His voice was gentle as he looked over at Graham, who stared back in disbelief.

"I stay here while you guys 'get her'?" Graham repeated the idea. "Michael, I'm –"

"I've seen how you are when it comes to her," Michael said firmly. "It's best if we don't do anything rash here."

"She's my best friend!" Graham protested, raising his voice. "I'm going –"

"You care for her more than that," Michael interrupted calmly. "We all know it, and we need to be rational. Someone needs to be able to get away if things go bad here. Not to mention the effects Gates have on non-Chosen. You won't be able to move, Graham –"

"I don't care!" Graham insisted angrily. "I'm going with you. Try to stop me."

For a tense moment, they stared each other down. Graham was slightly taller than Michael, and his eyes shone fiercely, challenging Michael. Liz looked between them, her stomach churning. She was anxious enough about what was to come without them turning on each other.

Finally, Michael looked away, his face expressionless. "Okay. I just hope your magic skills are more than good. Magic is all that will help us if we get into a fight."

Liz's heart dropped into her stomach. "I can't use magic."

Michael met her eyes. "What?"

"I've never been able to. I've tried and tried, but –"

"Best stick close to me then," Michael said grimly. "I'm not leaving you here."

"A minute ago you were trying to make *me* stay here!"

Graham pointed out irritably.

"You could defend yourself if you needed to," Michael said to him in a lowered voice, but Liz still heard him. "She's my sister. I'm not letting her out of my sight."

Graham met Michael's gaze for a few seconds and then nodded, turning back toward the valley. "We should go," he said softly, his eyes distant. "She's in there somewhere. We have to save her."

They made their way down the slope into the valley. Liz was still leading the way, her feet dragging. She hated everything about this. The main reason she'd even come with Michael and Graham was because she'd been too scared to stay with Sasha alone. She didn't want to die saving someone else – even if the someone else was Arabella, the girl who'd given up her entire life to save Liz. But even if she hadn't come with Michael and Graham, she would've ended up at the Gate sooner or later no matter what. With demons, the Alysparians... It seemed like facing Xanedur was inevitable. It always had been. But Liz was entirely unprepared for such a meeting. She wasn't even able to produce light, let alone use dark magic, and magic was what Michael had said would be the only thing effective against Xanedur.

She shook her head, trying to clear it, but it didn't work.

Suddenly everything went dark.

"You got your father's intelligence," a cold voice whispered. "Which isn't saying much." Liz opened her eyes but couldn't see anything for a few fearful moments. Then *she* appeared.

Out from the darkness, Liz's mother crept forward, so lightly that she might have been floating. Her eyes were as cold as her voice, her lips drawn in a smirk. Liz tried to take a step back, but all she could do was breathe.

"What are you doing to me?" Liz asked helplessly, internally struggling to move. But her muscles wouldn't respond, and Xanedur was quickly drawing closer.

"I have more control over you than you would've ever dreamt," Xanedur murmured. Though she was still several feet away, it sounded like she was speaking right next to Liz's ears.

"What do you mean?" Liz demanded, giving up on moving and trying to act calm and collected. *This isn't in the physical world, she can't hurt me*, Liz told herself repeatedly, trying to swallow her fear.

"You actually came to my Gate, you pathetic human," Xanedur crooned, coming close to Liz and appraising her critically. "What were you going to do? Talk me into letting you go? Into letting *her* go?"

"We're just–just–"

"Just what?" Xanedur scoffed. "Just playing right into my hands. You can't run now, but my child, how you should have tried."

"Why me?" Liz whispered, unable to control her tears any longer. "Why me, why not Michael? Why not ignore me completely? Why are you so determined to kill *me*?"

Xanedur's eyes grew hard, like icy-blue steel. "They were going to use you to kill me. My own daughter…as for why you instead of Michael? I tried to have him killed too, but then I found out that Cujan doesn't use 'sacrifices' like Alyspar does. Cujan wouldn't have used him against me, but Alyspar fully intended on using you. They will always try to use you. I can't risk being banished to the Other World. I'm not leaving the pleasures of this world." Her eyes glittered as she raised a hand to run it along the side of Liz's face. "My precious daughter..." For a moment, regret lingered in Xanedur's eyes.

"What if I joined you?" Liz begged in desperation, unable to even shiver at her mother's touch. "What if I helped you?"

"How could you possibly help me?" Xanedur asked pointedly. "Other than being eliminated before you can be used against me?"

"I could–I–" Liz couldn't think of anything she could do. A tear escaped her eye as it struck her how helpless, how useless, she was. She couldn't use magic. She couldn't take care of herself. She couldn't even help her demon mother in any way other than dying.

"Now," Xanedur declared decidedly, "it is time for you to go. My demons are taking Michael and Graham as we speak. You are surrounded in the physical world. All four of you will be killed, and then? I will be unstoppable."

Xanedur's form faded into mist, darkness taking over Liz's vision once again.

When she came to, she was indeed surrounded by demons. Large, humanoid shapes, dark as midnight, loomed around her. One of them reached toward her with long claws seemingly made of shadows, gripping her arm and roughly hauling her to her feet. She felt suddenly weak, as if that small meeting with Xanedur had taken a physical toll on her body.

Michael and Graham looked worn out as well, their feet dragging along the ground as demons forced them toward the cave where the Gate was. It was just barely visible to the searching eye at this point. The demon pinned Liz's arms behind her, pushing her toward the Gate...and Xanedur.

Why did we think this would work? Liz wondered, suddenly feeling numb and empty. This was it. This was where she would die. In just moments, her own mother would murder her, along with Michael, Graham, and Arabella. It felt so unfair that they had tried so hard to get here, and before they could even attempt to save Arabella, Xanedur had captured them.

As Liz continued with her despairing thoughts of her imminent death, they reached the cave opening. It was dark in the cave, having never been touched by the sun. It was almost as if traces of the Other World had seeped through the doors and into Liz's world. The demons hauled Liz, Michael, and Graham into the cave. Liz's eyes began to adjust to the darkness, and then uncontrollable fear settled in her chest.

The doors. There they were, the doors that had haunted Liz's dreams for as long as she could remember. The doors that had turned out to be a Gate to the Other World. Without consciously deciding to, she began to struggle against the demons' grips, crying out as panic set in. The demons growled and tightened their hold on her arms, one of them slapping her across the face when she didn't calm down. Subdued by the feeling of blood flowing down her face, she stopped squirming and let the demons take her toward the doors. She didn't look at Michael or Graham.

Just like in her vision, the Gate was set far back in the cave, opening onto a beautiful marble balcony with steps that hugged the cave wall all the way down to the ground. But unlike in her vision, there was something different. Xanedur stood on the balcony, staring down at them with a sick look of satisfaction. Finally seeing all of it in person, tears began to spill over out of Liz's eyes, mixing with the blood on her cheek, but she didn't feel herself crying. No sobs escaped her throat, no shivers passed through her body. Just tears, tracing their way down her cheeks and dripping to the ground. Michael and Graham hadn't even lifted their heads to look at the Gate. Though Liz couldn't see them well, she thought they must be unconscious.

Xanedur was in her human form, the form that looked so much like Liz. It made her stomach turn even more. She felt like she was looking at a mirror image. Xanedur turned and slowly made her way down the marble steps. The demons that had brought Liz, Michael, and Graham into the cave stopped, holding them still until Xanedur had reached the floor of the cave.

Liz's mother wore no shoes. Her hair was so dark that it looked blacker than black, and her eyes looked like they were made from ice itself. Her face was expressionless now. She wore a long, light purple gown with small rips and tears at the bottom. Then she spoke. Her voice was just as empty as it had been when Liz had seen her in her dreams.

"Rachel," Xanedur said pleasantly, as if greeting an old friend. She cast her eyes onto Michael and Graham, who remained unresponsive. "Levi. And Graham, whom I've heard so much about."

Liz tried to ask where Arabella was, but her voice was caught in her throat. She opened her mouth and then froze, the tears stil fresh in her eyes.

"Or should I call you Elizabeth and Michael?" Xanedur snarled mockingly, a look of anger coming over her face. "Leave them with me," she ordered the other demons, who were still holding them there. "Stay at the Gate. I can handle this." The demons hesitated before Xanedur snapped, "Go! I will call if I need you."

Obediently, the demons released Liz. When they let go of Michael and Graham, the two boys collapsed to the floor of the cave. The demons drifted up the marble steps and into the Gate. As they passed under the arched doorway, they disappeared into what just looked like a black wall. Xanedur watched them go.

Liz glanced at Michael and Graham. They both shuddered on the ground, curled up in balls. Liz saw now that they were awake, but their eyes were wide and unseeing.

"How pathetic," Xanedur whispered as she looked at them. "They can't even stand." She looked back at Liz, who did indeed feel a wave of weakness wash over her. But she was still able to stay on her own two feet. She met her mother's eyes apprehensively, wondering if it was too late to run. As the thought went through her head, Xanedur went on to say, "Some people can't handle being so close to a demon's Gate. So why are you still standing? And why is your half-demon brother, more adept at magic than you will ever be, hunched on the ground as if unable to move? What a joke..." Still looking bored, she turned and started to walk toward Michael with narrow, suspicious eyes.

At that moment, Michael's eyes hardened, and he jumped to his feet, his eyes shooting daggers at Xanedur. Before Xanedur could react, shadows erupted from Michael's hands, hitting her in the face. Her head became black mist for a moment before she dodged to the side, taken aback but obviously furious.

She advanced on Michael, staggering. "You imbecile!" she screeched, her voice sounding inhuman. Michael shot more shadows at her, but before they could hit her, she erupted into dark mist and flew up into the air. Shocked, Liz stared dumbly at the fight, her tears halting, her mouth still open.

And before she knew it, Graham was pulling himself up from the ground, obviously struggling against the power of the Gate and the near presence of the Other World. He got to his feet and began to stumble toward the marble stairs, far in at the back of the cave.

A shout from Michael caught Liz's attention. She spun around, eyes searching for Xanedur. Their demon mother was drifting around Michael's shots, streaking toward her brother, whose eyes were wide open with terror. Horrified, Liz reached out her hands together instinctively – she didn't know what she was trying to do – just as Xanedur was about to envelop Michael, and –

A dark lightning bolt flew forth from Liz's hands.

Chapter 21

THE SHADOW BOLT MOVED FASTER THAN LIGHT. BEFORE LIZ could process what had happened, Xanedur's misty form had halted, a gaping hole where the bolt had hit. Michael scrambled away from her in a panic, coming to Liz's side. He gave her an astonished sidelong glance. Liz blinked, in shock. Xanedur's form slowly came back together.

"You were never able to perform magic before," Xanedur hissed. "You insolent little –"

Michael, cutting her off, shot more shadows at her, running to keep himself between her and the entrance of the cave, prepared to flee. Though his shots were slower and less powerful than Liz's shadow bolt, they were enough to keep Xanedur distracted momentarily. Xanedur jumped to the side, again dodging Michael's shadows. Liz glaned at the base of the stairs, where Graham had collapsed, clinging to the rail in an attempt to climb the stairs.

Arabella.

Liz moved to rush over to help Graham up, but stopped in her tracks as Xanedur suddenly howled in anger, "Bring the girl out!" Liz, Michael, and Graham froze as a scream issued from the doors. Demons emerged from the Gate, hauling Arabella between them onto the balcony. "Keep her alive."

They were all silent save for Arabella, whose ragged breathing broke the silence. Graham stared intently at her, desperation in his eyes. Liz was stunned at Arabella's appearance. The former Princess, always so composed and capable, was now gasping for breath. Her eyes were wide, hair disheveled. Her clothes were torn. She'd obviously been roughtly handled in her time in the Other World. She met Liz and Michael's eyes in turn first, and then her eyes came to rest on Graham. She was quite clearly terrified out of her mind, almost to the point of hysteria.

Xanedur melted back into her human form, looking fondly at Arabella. "This one had quite the nerve," she said scornfully. "Pretending to be you when my ignorant demon workers came around. And actually fooling them, too! She had quite the fight in her at first, but that didn't last long. But one good thing came out of her taking your place... Now both of you are here." Her eyes scraped across Liz and Michael with an almost hungry glint in them. Xanedur went on to say, "Now, unless you want to die where you stand, you two–" her eyes threatened Liz and Michael, "–had better give yourselves up right now. Or do you want your precious Princess to die?"

"Let her go, please," Graham whispered. He was weak from being in the presence of the Gate. Without demon blood, the pressure from being near the Other World took a toll, both physically and mentally on him, and he was almost unable to speak.

"Not without these two," Xanedur said impatiently, gesturing to Liz and Michael. "How about a trade?"

Everyone was silent except for Arabella, still breathing heavily.

"Is that a no?" Xanedur asked slowly, narrowing her eyes.

Graham turned his hard eyes from Arabella to Liz and Michael. He considered them for many moments. Liz blinked, her heart sinking. They had all come to save Arabella together, but he was about to –

"You're not taking any of us," Graham growled, glaring at Xanedur. He forced himself to his feet. Arabella whimpered as the demon holding her twisted her arm.

"Fine then, have it your way." Xanedur watched them all for a moment in turn. "Kill them all," she finally ordered, turning back into black mist. As she seeped back into the air and toward the doors, the demon holding Arabella brought its claws up to her throat, prepared to strike.

"Arabella!" Graham shouted desperately. At the same moment, Liz shot darkness from her fingertips. The shadow bolt, poorly aimed, missed the demon and struck the cave wall. The demon jumped away from Arabella, throwing her to the floor of the balcony. Michael, eyes on Xanedur's misty form, raised his hands and shot lightning in her direction.

With a hiss, Xanedur took the hit and paused. "Fine. We'll do this the hard way." She started coming back toward Liz and Michael.

Graham was pulling himself up the stairs with a strained expression, trying with all of his might to reach Arabella. The former Princess had collapsed to the floor. Liz could hear her letting out small whimpers, but she couldn't focus on that right now. Xanedur was coming, slowly but surely.

Liz shot another shadow bolt at her mother, who managed to dodge it this time, speeding up until she was streaking through the air. Liz and Michael exchanged a glance for a split second before jumping out of the way in opposite directions. As they rolled to their feet, they turned toward Xanedur, raising their arms together and both firing shadows at the same time.

The shadows both hit Xanedur, and she let out a pained screech before shooting a shadow straight at Liz.

With a scream, Liz raised her arms to hide her face. This was it. This was where she died.

The shadow struck her arms, throwing her backward, but was deflected back toward Xanedur.

"How dare you!" Xanedur shrieked, her voice high, as the shadow bolt struck her misty form. It ruptured a hole that was quickly filled back up. But the cloud that was Liz's mother looked smaller than it had before being hit by two powerful shadow bolts.

With Xanedur momentarily dazed, Liz skidded to a stop by Graham's side at the base of the stairs, Michael at her heels.

Graham was staggering on the stairs, staring desperately at the top of the stairs.

"Arabella..." he mumbled before his legs gave out completely.

Michael frantically looked at Liz. "You get her!" he ordered. "I have to get Graham out of here!"

"What about Xanedur?" Liz gasped, looking over her shoulder at their mother's shadowy form as it came back together, her voice moaning in pain.

"We'll worry about her later. We have to get out of here!" Michael insisted, hoisting Graham to his feet. "Go!" he told her again when she didn't move. He stumbled under Graham's weight, but started to support him toward the cave entrance. Liz stared helplessly up the stairs for a moment, too terrified to move. Then she found her legs taking her up two steps at a time.

"Arabella!" she cried, reaching Arabella's side. Xanedur was growling in rage now, coming back together. "Arabella, we have to go!" Liz tugged at Arabella's limp arms. With a horrified glance at her mother, who was steadily growing more frightening with every passing second, Liz gave one last pull at Arabella. That seemed to waken her at last.

Arabella forced herself to her feet just as Xanedur snarled, "Stay away from my Gate!"

With her distracted, Michael and Graham had managed to get much closer to the cave entrance. With a jolt, Liz remembered that if enough of her blood was spilled in the Other World, Xanedur would die.

She didn't want to spill her own blood in the Other World to kill her mother.

She wanted out of this mess, and she wanted to hand it over to the more experienced Chosen of Cujan.

Liz and Arabella began to rush down the stairs, but Xanedur sped toward them and blocked their path, an intimidating misty shadow. She cackled maniacally, "You're not getting away that easily!"

Liz froze. There was only one way to go. Up.

Not thinking, she spun around and dashed up the stairs, back toward the Gate. With a furious shriek, Xanedur's form zipped over Arabella's head. Arabella flinched, cowering down with her hands over her head.

As soon as Xanedur was out of the way, Arabella, seeming stunned for just a moment, flew down the stairs and stumbled toward the cave entrance, joining Michael and Graham. But it was too late for Liz to turn back now, with Xanedur close behind her.

Liz had reached the balcony, Xanedur right on her heels. A crazy idea came to her in that split second. At the same time, Michael cried, "Liz!" and managed to shoot a shadow bolt at Xanedur.

As the rocks poured down from the ceiling where the shadow bolt had hit, Liz jumped through the doors, Xanedur letting out an angry growl behind her.

Chapter 22

"LIZ?" MICHAEL WHISPERED IN DISBELIEF, STARING AT the remnants of the Gate. The archway had crumbled to the ground. The darkness that had previously poured from the Gate was gone, and so were the doors. It looked as if there had just been a marble balcony leading to the wall, now covered in fallen boulders and rubble.

"No..." Arabella breathed, frozen. They all had their eyes glued to where, just seconds before, the doors had led to the Other World. Now... there were no doors at all. The Gate was broken, and Liz was gone.

"Where's Xanedur?" Graham demanded breathlessly. "She didn't –"

"She went in, too," Michael answered quietly, still in shock. He had been the one to shoot the shadow bolt. He'd been the one to destroy the Gate. He'd been the one who, despite vowing to protect her, had caused his sister to disappear.

Arabella moved her gaze over to Michael and Graham, where they stood by the entrance of the cave. Now that the connection to the Other World had been severed, Graham and Arabella were able to stand on their own feet. Sudden, silent tears escaped from Arabella's eyes. She rushed over to Graham, clinging to him with her head buried in his chest. She shivered with silent sobs. Graham, over her head, continued to watch smal rocks fall from the ceiling and walls of the cave.

It seemed like they'd been standing there for hours, waiting for Liz to reappear. Whether it had been that long or rather just mere seconds, none of them could tell. Michael eventually tore his eyes away from the broken Gate and looked at Graham and Arabella. She was still in his arms, now openly crying. Graham looked back at Michael with understanding eyes and gently pulled Arabella away from himself, meeting her eyes.

Michael jerked his head toward the entrance of the cave. "We should get out of here. We need to… do something."

Without any further words, they left the cave behind.

As soon as they'd gotten to the edge of the valley, looking back at the cave, now barely visible, they heard the sound of vehicles approaching. Too exhausted, shocked, and horrified to hide, they silently stood as Alysparians surrounded them, guns at the ready.

"Where's the Chosen?" the leader demanded harshly. When Michael, Graham, and Arabella didn't answer, simply staring blankly at him, he slowly lowered his gun with a look of confusion. "There were four. What... What happened?"

Graham and Arabella stayed quiet. Arabella's red, puffy eyes were filling with tears all over again, and Graham sniffed, trying to keep his own at bay. Michael, after a long look at his two companions, answered, "She ran into the Gate. With Xanedur."

The Alysparians exchanged dubious looks and rested their eyes on Michael again for a few seconds. Then they all lowered their guns. The lead Alysparian began questioningly, "So the Gate..."

"The Gate is gone. It was destroyed."

The Alysparian finally gestured for them to come toward the cars. "We'll take you as far as Fore. Our job... Our job is done, and you've been through enough. We won't hurt you. Not even you two fugitives," he added to Graham and Arabella hesitantly. "The Queen doesn't need to know that we saw you."

They didn't care enough to think. They went with the Alysparians.

When they'd reached the small town on the Cujan border, the Alysparians dropped them off. "We're no longer welcome here," the leader said apologetically. "This is as far as we can go. We must return to the Queen and tell her what's happened."

Michael, Graham, and Arabella made their way to a phone booth, and Michael called someone. Graham and Arabella didn't care who it was at this point, nor did they pay attention to what he was saying. Arabella's eyes were no longer wet with tears as she held tightly onto Graham's arm.

"We're set," Michael said listlessly. "They'll take us to the Cabinet so we can... report what Alyspar's been doing with the Chosen." When Graham and Arabella looked at him with no expressions, he added, "That's all we can do at the moment. Right now, we need to find a hotel to stay the night in. Someone will be here in the morning."

They settled in at a nice hotel, Michael apparently putting the charges on some unknown tab. Without speaking, they reached their room, and each one sat, looking lost.

"All of that for nothing." Arabella's voice was quiet. It was the first time she'd coherently spoken since they'd left the Gate. With Graham's arm securely around her shoulders, she said, "We rescued her from my mom so she wouldn't get killed. And now..." She trailed off, looking at nothing.

She turned toward Graham and snuggled into his side, holding off more tears. He held her comfortingly, but he still hadn't said much since they'd left the Gate either.

At some point, they all laid down to rest.

They groggily woke up one by one, blinking open wide eyes.

"Was that real?" Arabella murmured to Graham, though she already knew the answer. He didn't respond. Still not expecting anyone to reply, she went on, "Is she really... dead?"

Michael had been awake for a while now, sitting on the

edge of the bed and facing away from them. Hearing her rhetorical questions, he turned back to them, looking thoughtful and confused.

"You're not going to believe this," he said slowly, pausing for a moment as he considered the floor. "But... She's not dead."

"What?" Graham and Arabella demanded at the same time, giving him doubtful looks.

He met their eyes in turn. "When I was asleep, I could feel it... Her presence... She's alive. She's stuck there." He looked back at the floor. "Liz is stuck in the Other World."

Epilogue

THE SOUTHERN PEAKS ROSE IN FRONT OF THEM, A WELCOME sight to Liam's eyes. He was so close to home. Then, with a flutter in his chest, he remembered that Koln had been burnt to the ground by the demons. His mother had been killed.

Looking up with determination, he considered the Southern Peaks again. His mother may have been killed, but his father, Milon, was still alive. And Liam was going to find him.

The Queen had let him go, free from his status as a fugitive after he'd revealed the location of Liz, Graham, and Arabella. His false sister had made a selfish decision, he kept telling himself. She'd run away instead of accepting who she was as one of the Chosen. Now, Liam was going to find out exactly who he was himself by finding Milon. His father would explain, he would help Liam understand.

Accompanied by Prince Thomas, who'd gladly taken up

the chance of getting out of Aloria and into the mountains again, Liam made his way toward the last known location of Milon. It was a broad area, and it would almost certainly take time to find him, considering the fact that no one had seen him in a little more than a decade. But Liam wanted answers.

Liam insisted on walking in front of the rest of the small group. Most of the others were on horses, but after his journey from Koln to Aloria with Seth and Liz, Liam felt like he'd had enough horseback riding for quite a while. The soft clopping of hooves gained on his heels, but he didn't even look at Prince Thomas as he caught up to him.

"Liam, we need to rest," Thomas informed him gently. "I understand that you want to find him, but everyone can't keep going like you can. I'm actually impressed you haven't fallen over from exhaustion yet. You've been walking for hours now."

"And I"m not stopping," Liam snapped, not caring if he was rude to the Prince. "You guys can rest. Catch up to me. I'm going to find my dad."

They'd clearly had this argument before. Thomas dropped it with a sigh. He went back to the rest of the group, calling out for them to set up a small camp that would give them a few hours to rest. Liam continued to walk alone, the voices and laughter falling out of his earshot eventually. He preferred being alone at this point anyway. There was no one to lie to him here.

He made his way up the side of a steep slope, reaching the trees and foothills of the Southern Peaks. At the top of the slope, he felt his feet slip, and he lost his balance. Panic overcame him as he started to fall down, a harsh tumble inevitable. A steady hand caught him until he'd regained his balance. Alarmed, he spun around to see who'd saved him from what would have certainly been a painful start to his search. But he had a welcome feeling that his search was already over.

A short, stout man faced Liam, his skin a tan color with wavy blond hair and deep, brown eyes. Liam knew exactly who this man was just from looking at him. The man gave him a friendly smile, which he returned with the satisfied words, "Hey, Dad."

END